MY STORY OF Resilience FROM MY VILLAGE

ANGELINAH C. BONIFACE KEGAKILWE

This book is a publication of
Billionaire Publishers
billionairepublishers.zim@gmail.com

Editing and Typesetting by Marshal Chiza
Proof Reading by Brian Muradzikwa
Book Cover Design by Diligent Palmer

Printed by Billionaire Publishers (Bulawayo , Zimbabwe)

Dedication

To my mother, my Proverbs 31 woman, for all you had to endure for me to be the woman I am today. I am forever grateful. To my father, may your soul find rest; Mhofhu. To my children, grandchildren, and great-grandchildren, may this be our timeless connection.

Endorsements

Dedication and remarkable service to Humanity is what makes Angie an inspiration to all of us. She is solemn about culture and is not afraid to help lead the next generations, even through painful life experiences.

Mainza Kangombe: *Founder, Kangombe.org*

In Branded, Angie takes us on a girl child's journey through adversity, fear, uncertainty, hope, despair and perseverance to triumph and adulthood. It is a self-portrait in which we can all appreciate the common humanity in diverse cultures as well as the cultural contradictions that provide both nurturing and warmth while also hiding abuse and oppression. It is the story of a young girl growing up in a small village in rural Botswana whose determination and dream of a better life took her from poverty to the world stage of an international public servant.

Dr. Onalenna Selolwane: *Former Professor of Sociology,*
University of Botswana

Here is hope for young girls who may find themselves facing challenges that threaten their dreams and those who find themselves having to make difficult choices that may at face value appear rebellious when in fact sits at the very core of transforming their lives, purposeful rebellion, especially where culture remains integral to ways of lives.

Moncho Kebonyethebe Moncho: *Social activist*

Angie's story of resilience is a powerful reminder that your limits are not defined by where you come from. *Branded* is a compelling anecdote about overcoming life's challenges as a teenage mother in rural Africa to becoming an influential force in International Civil Service.

Nosipho Dhladhla: *International Civil Servant*

Contents

Foreword

Life is a journey. Life can depress, drive, enthuse and ignite hope. That expedition when told will always have an impact on others. There are many life stories out there that have been told, that have been sung about. Nonetheless, there are those documented which we can positively learn from and inspire us. We can learn from Angie's story! It is an African story in an African setting that deals with adversity, rekindling drive, raising passion and instilling hope.

It is a story about how a person who is enmeshed in the complexities of immigration, tribal feuds, competing religions, regressive cultural inhibitors and socio-economic lethargies can rise from singing songs of despair to leading a chorus of a symphony that exuberates the audiences. It conveys a dream-like realistic-naturalistic depiction of the biblical prophecy of Prophet Ezekiel's "vision of the dry bones". The story teaches us that any dreams, ambitions, and aspirations that have been reduced to nothing could rise again. It tells us that with personal inner power and faith in God's hand, one can resurrect their "dead dreams". Yes, the story is here - your dry bones too can rise again! It is a story of the resilience of a naïve young girl starring at helplessness, disentangles from it, turns this into a positive path and rises from the ashes like a noble eagle in its flight! It is a story of how a teenage mother can comprehend that the limitations she faces are not an infinite condemnation and searches her mind, feelings, historical breaches, structural unfairness and systemic bias to rise again!

This story has one central focus on education as a driver, enabler, liberator of the mind and great social equalizer in an African environment. We learn through Angie's story that on the crest of education you can pursue diligence and dine with Kings and Queens. We learn that no matter wherever you are in the social echelons, to work hard at education can produce diligent hands that bring wealth of knowledge to deal with glaring poverty. I believe Angie's story demonstrates that education is a means to constantly challenge and recreate the world so as to restore human dignity.

The story says education is a public good that can light the feet of the disadvantaged. It can make one stand on a pedestal and peep in the future with certainty. Education can make one have a predictive value that will enable them to strive to be a player and not a pawn in the global equation. Clearly, this story shows that with a mark of excellence, beyond intellectual nourishment, education can remodel one into a tour of duty beyond their defined home to translate knowledge into realism and solve global challenges. It also can create true leadership in opinion, thought, character, words and deeds. I believe, as others do, that the empires of tomorrow are those of the mind and that knowledge is the axis on which our current and future status will revolve.

Lastly, we also learn that there is a spiritual intimation for success in this world. In the world order that tends to musk unfair dispensations and deep social disorder, this story unravels how, in combination with other factors, spiritual faith in God can relieve the constant human pain in order to restore humanity and collectivity in a society riddled with unbridled individualism and competition. It invokes that spiritual dimension which can restore the real purpose for life in the shades of despair!

To me, this is indeed a story about how a person that has passion and drive can search and find a hero in themselves. This story has inspired me but is should also particularly inspire those girls and young female citizens of Africa and the world, that in the face of all adversity, there is always an alternative of possibilities. We should all strive to bring the best of our human abilities for the betterment of the world.

So, go search for a hero in yourselves! Long live the resilient spirit of Angelinah Boniface!

Prof Trywell Kalusopa
University of Namibia, Namibia

Introduction

I was born a foreigner in a beautiful African village called Moroka, a very small village situated in the eastern part of Botswana. It shares a border with four other small villages; Ramokgwebana, Kgari, Jackalas No.1 and Mapoka. To the north, Moroka village also shares a border with the Republic of Zimbabwe, former Southern Rhodesia. This makes Moroka very unique in many ways. Moroka village is the primary setting for my story. Its proximity to Zimbabwe bears deep roots in the trajectory of my life journey and my family history.

Allow me to take you through the beauty of my village as I marvel yet again, at the place I have felt most at home. Moroka village radiates an aura of peace and serenity as birds chirp and villagers diligently work or walk leisurely on the single main road that cuts across the village. It is in this main road, the small dusty alleys and the walkways meandering and sprouting all over the village where I became me. It is on these streets where we as teens, would idle, looking for attention or trouble. Incidentally, this is the main road linking the villages to the surrounding fields, cattle posts that provide arable farming and the mainstay of the local economy. The road also connects the village with our nearest city, Francistown and the municipal administration village of Masunga.

There is an absence of street lights, traffic lights, roundabouts, or pedestrian crossings. We have long, curvy, narrow streets cutting beautifully through the village as one village connects to the other. Most of the drama that happened in the villages most likely happened on these dusty alleys. This includes early childhood fights, first kisses, first make-outs, first breakups and everything in-between. Anything interesting that could ever happen, happened on Moroka Main Road.

The vast beauty of Moroka village is further defined by the surrounding fauna and flora that meanders through a gentle topography. A few mountains and rocks surround the village and there are two rivers that cut across, dividing the neighbourhood on both ends. These small mountains are seen on the western and northern parts of the village as they declare the glory of the universe. It is however, the villagers of Moroka who make the village a marvel.

From the south or west, you can feel the peace and serenity that surges through the veins reminding you that this place is different. This is home.

I cannot be defined outside my village; it is the core of my being. To understand me is to step onto these dusty catwalks of Moroka. I have run on these dusty streets, carefree, barefooted, playing with my friends and doing my chores. I recall fetching water for my mother from the nearby community standpipe and carrying that bucket of water on my head as my mother worked to place food on the table. We had no running water, neither did we have electricity or proper plumbing yet the essence of life was more tangible here than anywhere else. To this day, this village remains my happy place.

Weekends are a great time in Moroka village. The people actually observe weekends. People stay at home or go to the cattle post. Others hang around at the local pub, idling there for no reason.

To provide context, one must observe that Batswana (people from Botswana), live in four types of homesteads, which are, the village, the city, the cattle post and the farm. As herders and cultivators, the Tswana found the high plains to their liking, because the grass was excellent for cattle and the soil was deep and easy to cultivate. Sorghum, beans, pumpkins, sweet melons and gourds were planted. However, the combination of people and animal farming did not work well, hence the division between farms and the cattle post. During the ploughing season, people would move to the farm until the harvest period had elapsed. The cattle post or "moraka" is solely for ranch farming.

The village is the perennial home especially for those who have no farms or cattle posts. Thus it became the place where amenities like schools, hospitals and post offices could be built.

However, this was disrupted by the development of cities. With urbanisation came the fourth homestead, that is, the city. I grew up in the village whereas others can relate either to masimo or moraka. Masimo being the farm and moraka being the cattle post.

I now live in New York City where the "I love NYC" sign is everywhere. When I see this sign, I always replace it with Moroka. "I love Moroka". This is home. Home is what unites us. Home is where my heart is.

Why This Book and Why Now?

"There is no greater agony than bearing an untold story inside you."
Maya Angelou.

Every life is a story and every story is a lesson. Every lesson, every story is an opportunity for us to be better. A life story can show us what we have the potential to become. It can inspire and encourage us. Stories give hope, so this book offers hope with the story that it weaves about my experiences.

Here is mine.

I became a mother at sixteen, a school dropout and an outcast. Coming from a religious sect that did not allow formal education, it was a long road to the ivy league schools. Fast forward to today, I am the first in my family to go to high school; first to graduate at Ivy League University, first to hold a master's degree; first to live abroad and even first to fly on the airplane.

It is this perseverance that I thought can inspire other girls who may be going through the same predicament that I went through in life. Never lose hope. You are not your circumstances. Circumstances, tragedies, and situations are the journey to becoming. Fall in love with the journey. Fall in love with process. Never miss an opportunity to learn from your experiences.

Among the many lessons I learnt as a teenage mother is that my story is my own and I can choose which narrative it should follow. I was born and raised in the village by poor parents who had little formal education. Their strict religious beliefs were embedded in our way of living and we were a society mired in prejudice. Life was monotonous and for many, destiny was carved from birth. This is a truth that I refused to accept early in life.

Preconceived expectations of society concerning who I was to become, have always been prevalent. There was a clear-cut perspective of life that was reinforced as the norm and I, like everyone else, was supposed to flawlessly abide to it. For me and other females, this norm emphasized the following pattern: grow up, get married; be an exemplary wife; bear many children and raise them to be responsible citizens of the society that raised you.

In other words, I was pre-destined to be an obedient wife, a humble mother and a respectable member of society with little or no formal education, who would sell vegetables at the local market to assist her husband in providing for the family.

This was in essence, the prescription of my grandfather's religious beliefs.

As part of our religious beliefs, I was not to mix with the gentiles or acquire their education because we were the "chosen generation." In fact, this meant that by being born into this religious sect, with all these prescriptions, my life was already BRANDED.

The principle at the centre of our lifestyle was that we were a pure and chosen generation and God expected us to live without blemish. Mixing with the outside world was contamination and contamination would require cleansing for one to be accepted back into the community.

We were expected to be entrepreneurial and not seek formal employment as integration into the 'other world' was seen as compromise. These were the beliefs of my grandfather's faith, Johane we Masowe, which was founded in Zimbabwe.

It is however, amazing that despite being unable to read and write, most members of our community had excellent entrepreneurial skills. They could drive, build houses and even fix cars. This group of people was one of the most creative and innovative in the country. In Moroka village, my people are known as Bazezuru. If anything needed to be done, the Bazezuru were the Silicon Valley of the village. They made their utensils out of iron. They ploughed, fed the village from their backyard gardens and gave colour to the village by their white regalia.

My father too as a Mozezuru, was a jack of all trades. He built houses despite never having attained any formal engineering or construction education. Everything he knew and did, he had taught himself and with time and experience, he had perfected his art.

I had a cousin who did Design and Technology at middle school. One day I listened to this dialogue after my father had caught him doing some handy work.

Dad: Ravu, how many tools do you need for such a small job?

Ravu: Safety first uncle. There are too many risks. We need to ensure that health and safety are at the core of our craft. This is D&T 101.

Dad: I built all this village with only this overall I am wearing and this wooden ladder. I do not need anything else.

Ravu: This ladder is not even safe. All the nails are hanging on it.

Dad: Why would you put your foot on the nail? Just climb the ladder and forget the nail. Leave the nail alone.

There are many such conversations between my cousin and my father as they tried to show each other who was smarter at their craft. I saw the change in generational mind-sets and ways of doing things. My father was of the older generation while Ravu and I were the new breed with different ways of doing things. My father always thought he was or could be the best Design and Technology teacher in the village. He would always invite my brother to come with him to his worksites to learn hands-on. I am not sure how that went, but it surely did amount to much as Daggie, my brother, is still to build a house. He never had any interest in climbing ladders. He however, loved cars. He loved to drive but he did not like building houses.

My confusion related to the church policy of shunning formal work, arose from the fact that although we were "a chosen generation", poverty had already left a mark in our genes. Some things failed to make sense. I knew then from a young age, that something was not right and I also knew that something had to change. I did not know what it was then, but I think I know better now.

We were more fortunate than most families in our sect because my father was a great advocate of sending children to school. To this day, my father remains my greatest hero. I call him, 'the Legend'.

This is what I am certain of; "God empowered me to empower others, especially my generation". God empowered me to empower them because I was one of them. I am the bridge. I am the bridge towards the ideal anyone in my family can aspire to achieve. In my process of becoming me, I had to break generational curses. I had to break the chains of poverty, pain, and illiteracy.

One could question what life experiences I had that are worth sharing. My response is that "every life is a story that is woven by every single experience we endure. There is therefore no story too youthful or too old to hold no value for each has its own lessons. Each deserves an audience."

In a world of unrelenting changes, uncertainty and unprecedented circumstances, this book offers a word of encouragement to that young girl who might think that the predicament that ensnares her today is permanent. The book is meant for that girl who has been told countless times that she is neither good enough nor pretty enough by a society that can sometimes seem unforgiving. To all the labelled and branded girls alike, this is meant to prompt you and awaken your spirit to another light of hope.

The book is here to remind the reader that any present circumstances that might inspire doubt, should never define who you are or who you become. Circumstances are lessons to make you better and stronger. And no matter what society says, you can choose your own path to be who you want to be. You are not people's perceptions, and you are not your circumstances. You alone are worthy. You are who you choose to be. Choose wisely.

It is my strong belief that it does not matter where we are born, how we grow up, or what circumstances we are in now, we are only going through a process that prepares us to be the best versions of ourselves. Savour the process.

More importantly, there is also the saying that a nation with no history is lost. And I say, a family that cannot trace its history is lost.

I come from an oral history society. Hence this book is my connection to future generations.

I hope my story inspires your story.

Part 1

THE DIVERSITY AND BEAUTY OF HOME

The village huts smell of damp wood and exemplify a modest lifestyle. Trees tower over the entire village. Their broad, green leaves providing shade from the radiant sun. Dusty pathways wind throughout the village providing direction to the different corners of the village.

Moroka Village

The village of Moroka according to village standards in Botswana, is modern and upscale. The beauty, the tranquillity, the peace and calm, are felt through its astoundingly beautiful sunrises and sunsets. It was such a joy rising up in the morning as each new day ushered in new hope, another beginning and plenty of dreams.

Botswana as a whole has been blessed as her days are made known by the brilliance of sunshine and cobalt skies. This beauty is almost perennial. The night skies are as exquisitely diamond-studded as the Kalahari sands. The sunsets in Moroka are nature's marvel and one should endeavour to experience them first-hand. One learns to appreciate this setting especially after they have been so far away from it.

This is what caused my initial shock when I first landed in Sheffield in the United Kingdom. My senses could not comprehend my immediate environment and for a short while, I felt lost. For the first time in my life, I could not use my shadow to determine what time it was. It was strange not knowing from which direction the sun rose, let alone being unable to see the sunsets.

Growing up, the sun played a crucial role as it was as good as the clock. I knew when to get up and reach school on time based on sunrise. Regardless of which season, everyone knew that once the sun was seen over the head, it was an indication that it was midday.

My grandmother knew by looking at the shadows of the huts as well as hers what time it was. It was the beauty of growing up in the village. We had a watch, but we could hardly afford the battery to operate it as it was considered a luxury. The wall clock ended up as a wall decor as it did not work most of the time. The sun, therefore, was the only reliable clock.

Apart from the beautiful modern homes which bring a sense of pride to this village, there is also an absence of the hum and bustle of traffic. Here, only wind and birdsongs are heard. This is the air that one can breathe without wheezing and hacking and allergies are unknown.

3

Moroka evenings are usually quiet except for the odd cars driving along the main road. Our local train station is two miles away. This is where the trains connect Botswana with neighbouring Zimbabwe and cut through the village. It is not the most reliable mode of transport, but we are grateful it is available. In fact, I can hardly remember the last time the train passed through Ramokgwebana station. One can only hope that one day, the railroad will be improved.

There is little entertainment in the village except for the local pub. It is a communal place for interaction and gossip. There were few other diversions as television-watching was rare as well as highly monitored.

We are delighted when we see guests. The arrival of guests sparks celebration and feasting. There is a local proverb that says, "Moeng goroga, dijo di bonale," which means, "Let the visitor arrive, and dinner will fix itself." Refusing a meal that is offered is regarded as a great offense. Even for the passing neighbour, it is courteous and expected that one always offers them some tea.

That was my worst nightmare, having to fix tea for each passing guest. This meant keeping the fire going on most days or sometimes we had to start a fresh fire as one guest left and another arrived. Cooking with firewood wasn't the easiest thing. Also, making sure there was enough supply of firewood

4

rested on me as the girl of the family. If I wasn't making tea for visitors, I was in the bush fetching firewood. During rainy seasons, it was extremely hard as the wood would be wet.

The two rivers that flow through the village served as the communal swimming pools. Also, our backyards were the best playgrounds as they provided the space to mingle with friends and have fun. When schools were closed, we played from dawn to sunset around the village.

The practice of locking doors or worrying over security was unknown to us. No one, not even mothers, ever got anxious about their children's whereabouts. It was not unusual for me to leave home at dawn and return at dusk after having spent the day with friends or nearby relatives. I enjoyed sleepovers at my friends' or my cousins' places. A child belonged to the village. If I was not playing with my stuffed plastic dolls and mash toys, I would be playing teacher at the back of my mother's house with lines of buckets as students.

I used to take sticks of left-over chalks from school and turn the walls of our house into a chalkboard as I played teacher. This was obviously to the displeasure of my mother. My writings could be seen in every room in the house. This is how I knew I was a teacher at heart. When I learnt something, I was very excited to share it with others. I loved to see their joy when they felt what I had experienced after learning something new. Those were the most fulfilling moments of my childhood.

If I opted not to play teacher to my make-believe class, I would easily be found playing at my friend's place. We had a variety of games to keep us busy, such as hide and seek, blackjack and mmantwane, which is a game of playing "house." We built homes and food out of mud. It was fun because I got to choose who could play my husband and my children. It was a delight to decide what we could pretend to cook and have "family meals". This was a reflection of our community at the unit level and we harnessed what teachings were expected of us girls as we grew older.

As playful as we were, there was hardly time to go home and eat. It was therefore amazing that our community had such an embracing attitude towards all children. This meant that we would eat food wherever we were playing. These were some of my fondest memories. It is not hard to see and accept that a child belonged to everyone. We were encouraged to share food from the same plates and this strengthened our bonds. In our village, everyone was family. It was the best childhood one could hope for.

Without any doubt, it is the countryside that steals one's heart and captures one's imagination. Wherever people gather, they love to eat, drink, sing and make music. There is plenty of talented singers and most people can easily be enticed into song. It is a place where you can attend a wedding and partake of the feast without knowing either the groom or the bride. One simply brings a chair and becomes part of the celebration. There is a joke that the food served at funerals is usually so good that most people attend funerals to have a share of the food. It is therefore common that when people are eating, one person might even ask fellow mourners if anyone knew the deceased. This is us. There is a joke we also used to make about funerals. Funerals are very sacred in Botswana. We bury our own with respect and dignity. People travel from far to pay their last respect to the departed. The popular and famous the person was, the bigger the numbers of people in attendance and the "cars". Before I get to the joke, let me tell you about funerals in Botswana.

It is a norm that every weekend there is a funeral going on. Sometimes even multiple funerals in the same village. Because each village has its own burial site, you may have three or more burials each weekend at the cemetery.

In Botswana, when a person dies, the whole village rallies and supports the family with the preparations for burial. And, there is a lot of preparations depending on the culture and religious beliefs of the deceased. We bury mainly weekends to give everyone who knew the person to pay their last respects.

From the day the person dies until the weekend when the body is finally buried, the family and community go into mourning.   Depending on the culture and religion of the family, there are prayer services held every evening at the family's compound until the burial. These services serve as comfort and a remembrance of the deceased. Speakers would at these serves offer spiritual uplifting words and console the family. Throughout the weeks, all the rituals and norms are performed until burial on Saturday or Sunday.

The day before the burial, usually a Friday, is a big day. It is the memorial service day. This is also the day when the body of the deceased is picked up from the morgue and spend the night in the home for the last time before the final home. This is a very sacred process. There are certain people who are selected to go pick up the body at the morgue. A convoy of cars will bring the departed home.

Growing up in the village, I had seen most of these envoys. The feeling is eerie, so real and stays forever in your mind. This convoy arrives usually in the evening. As child it's a little scary. So, if this convoy finds you on the road, the norm is for one to sit down, kneel on the road, until the cars pass, as a sign of respect to the departed. One can only continue with their journey once the whole convoy has passed.

On Friday, men in the community will go to the graveyard to help the family dig a grave for the burial. While this is going on other community members, mostly women, will come and help assist with cooking for the next day. Remember the food I mentioned earlier. This food is prepared the night before. The amount of food cooked, and cows killed depends on the socioeconomic status of the family. Friday evening there is one last memorial service. Bodies are always buried and never cremated. Most people are buried in caskets.

On the same Friday, usually around 10pm there will be a prayer service called tebelelelo. This prayer service lasts all night long till the wee hours of the morning. During the service people pray and mourn for the deceased. While the service is on, some women and men are off preparing food for the next day. The men will be cooking the slaughtered oxen and goats and the women will be making tea.

Around 1 or 2 am people stop mourning to have some tea and bread. Then around 3am more prayers, words of encouragement and consolation are said and then the community continues with their mourning. At 5am the coffin is opened, and people are allowed to go in to see the body and say any last words to the deceased. 6:30am Saturday morning there is one last service before heading to the burial grounds. Here relatives, friends and co-workers talk about the decreased and explain how he died. The deceased family members will read any messages people wrote to be buried with the casket. Then the casket is decorated with the messages and flower arrangements. Some songs are singing, and more prayers are said. In most cases church members of the deceased will come dressed in robes to help run the service and the burial proceedings. Once this is done the casket will be carried to the hearse. Then there will be another convoy of cars to the cemetery.

Everyone is allowed to the come and witness the final burial. For us, this is a sacred process. In the program for the service, there is actually a person called "rra dikolo" meaning director of car services. Just like there is a Master of Ceremonies, there is a director of cars. We take this process serious, e.g the second car in the convoy is always the car carrying the casket. This process reminds of the secret service detail for the president of the United States. We have the diluted version of that process when it comes to our funerals. It's not air force one or marine one, its car service one.

The joke for village girls was that, when village girls get to the town, and the see traffic jam, they should not sit down all day thinking it's a funeral.

In my country and particularly in Moroka, when people want to identify you, they ask about the section of the village where you were born and who your parents are and then dig into every shred of evidence that may prove that you are a relative

Everyone is related in one way or the other, just by being born in Moroka. This is a place where, when people ask how you are doing, they mean it. They stop their business and errands to actually ask about how you and your family are doing. The smiles here are genuine. There is no grin. We laugh out loud.

In Botswana, let alone Moroka, most families survive on subsistence farming which includes keeping cattle. The beef industry has played a great role in the economy of the country. There are more beef cattle in Botswana than there are people. It must be one of the few countries in the world where beef is cheaper than chicken.

MOROKA AND HER DIVERSITY

The village largely derives its beauty from its inhabitants and there is no village in Botswana which is as rich in diversity as my home village.

It is believed that the Kalangas and the Ndebeles, who originate from Zimbabwe's Matebeleland, were the original settlers. They settled in Moroka before the erection of the borders between the two countries. The next to settle were the royal ethnic tribe of the Barolong and the last to arrive were the BaZezuru of Mashonaland, Zimbabwe. The Bazezuru is my tribe and it is believed they arrived in the early forties. The richness and diversity of Moroka village transcend race, religion, culture, and philosophy. I have to admit, I learnt the beauty of diversity and integration at a very young age from growing up in this unique village. This is why settling in a cosmopolitan environment comes easily to me since I grew up amid rainbows.

Even the neighbouring villages surrounding Moroka, do not have a wider array of tribes as we do. Throughout all my travels around the world, I have never struggled to understand the differences in cultures. I may struggle to settle at the beginning, but I adjust very quickly. I am very flexible when it comes to tolerating and embracing other cultures. I have learnt that there is beauty in diversity and that being different should be our point of power. We may come in different shades and shapes, but at the core, we are all the same. This is the gift of acceptance that was bestowed on me by my village.

Three different ethnic groups have lived in harmony for over sixty years. The three ethnic tribes speak three different languages. They have three different cultures. Their beliefs and ways of life are different, yet we have survived and thrived together. The Barolong speak Serolong, which is their native dialect derived from Setswana. Setswana is one of the official languages together with English.

The Barolong are the leaders and the more prominent tribe in the village since it is the royal tribe. The Kalanga is the second most prominent and they make up the larger proportion of the village population. They speak Kalanga, which is a language closer to Shona since both are Zimbabwean dialects. We are the baZezuru who speak Shona and we are the minority.

Life may not be perfect, however, the people of Moroka are the happiest people I have ever seen. I have lived in the United Kingdom, Europe, and the United States, but these cannot compare with Moroka.

13

Diversity breeds humanity in people and society stands to gain if it learns to appreciate the richness of our differences, empathise and focus more on what makes us unique, rather than on what divides us.

GOING BEYOND UNCONSCIOUS BIAS

As a society, we are still entangled in a predicament of discrimination deriving from diversity. This is foreign to Moroka. The notion that differences in appearance, belief, or way of life, make one person better than another, is indeed fickle. We formulate assumptions that make us judge, avoid, or act awkwardly towards people who are different from us. These assumptions are based on fear of the unknown because of our uninformed biases against a group of people. These are nothing but perceptions.

If we could take time to learn about and understand each other on a deeper level, it would save us the pain and heartache that are a result of our uninformed judgements. Facts matter and being informed matters. I find the attitude that it-is-them-or-us to be very counter-intuitive.

Fear of difference spawns racism, hatred, animosity, and keeps societies apart. We have disconnected ourselves from the depth of our souls. Instead of connecting with our hearts, we are using our minds to divide us. There is a need to emphasise that we are stronger because of our differences. Our differences allow us to widen our horizons. Ultimately we are one people deserving of acceptance, understanding, respect and love. Everyone thrives and blossoms in the affirmation of one-ness. We all want to feel valued and wanted. We should all focus on this. The uniqueness you will find in Moroka village is heart-warming. It is not perfect but it offers plenty of happy moments or experiences.

Growing up in this little rural village taught me that life is a shared communal journey where we all should strive to see each other as one. The sweet and beautiful memories linger. This is the place where no matter how far I go, it will always stay in my heart.

Early Childhood with a Difference

There was something different about growing up in the Bazezuru compound of Moroka Village. Remember I mentioned earlier, I am a Mozezuru belonging to the Bazezuru tribe. This is where my story begins, in the Bazezuru compound.

The Bazezuru were a special species. We all lived in a big compound within the village. Everyone had their yard within the compound. It looked to me like a huge camping site without tents, only brick and mortar. There were no white picket fences or hedges, however, somehow everyone seemed to know where their yard started and ended. We had small gardens around the compound to grow basic vegetables and fruits. There was also a public standpipe for running water. I spent most of my youth at this standpipe, where I would mingle with friends.

Everything about Bazezuru centred on religion and faith. Religion is a way of life. It dictated the way we lived and how we engaged with each other. We had our norms, values, and indeed our culture. We spoke a different language. We had a different dress code, and above all, we had a religion that permeated our way of life.

The daily routine revolved around the church. From daily morning and evening prayers to all-day Saturday prayers, we were different. Not hearing the preacher man at 5:30am calling for morning prayers would mean that there was either a death in the compound or something disturbing had happened. This was the only time when the morning and evening prayers were suspended. It was a ritual that showcased our dedication and obedience to the spiritual calling. The preacher's call was also a clock or an alarm, signalling the beginning or end of the working day.

Although we were in the compound, there was something that was clear and has never changed in my mind and that is diversity can never be confined. We may try to exclude ourselves and create our own identity, yet diversity is bigger than our imagination.

My friends who lived outside the compound would play with me on weekdays and Sundays. On Saturdays, no outsiders were allowed in the compound since it was observed as a holy day. Saturday was the ultimate day of prayer and worship. It was indeed the holy Sabbath. If you were not part of the church, you could not enter the compound. An exception was only when there was death inside the compound, and people from outside were allowed to attend the funeral.

I looked forward to weekends because of the quietness and calmness that prevailed in the compound. People did not do any chores except to cook for their families. It was a break for me from the routine of having to fetch water for our garden or for the household.

The irony is that my father had ceased to observe the practice because he now had his own different views. However, since we were living in the compound, on Sabbath days when my cousins were at church, I would remain behind. But I would often sneak out of the compound and play with my friends who lived outside the compound. This was not allowed, and I would have received corporal punishment had I been discovered by the pastors. It did not matter that we were not active at church, it only mattered that we were part of the sect. So all my outings were discreet. As my double life continued to reveal itself, I began to question issues at a very young age. Here are the questions I struggled with:

Who really am I? Who is everyone else? (around me, the compound and outside). How do I fit into the puzzle? And most importantly, does it matter?

The people in the compound were of the Christian sect that had seen my grandfather embarking on a mission around Africa, spreading the gospel, planting churches until he finally decided to settle in Moroka Village. My grandfather had passed on before I was born. If I had met him, certainly I would also have had so many questions for him. My first question to him would have been, "How do you feel? How does it feel to have lived half of your life on this earth as an immigrant? Most of all, what have you learnt about humanity?"

For some reason, I see myself in my grandfather's story, which makes me believe that migration is indeed in my blood. There is a phenomenon called generational patterns. I think migration would pass as a generational pattern for my family. My grandfather left Zimbabwe as a young man in search of his calling. I left Botswana as a young woman in search of education. I never thought my life would turn out that way.

What I am certain of is that to understand my life journey, and hopefully make sense of it, I would need to get back to the beginning. It started with my grandfather's story.

MISSIONARY ORIGINS:
BORN AS AN IMMIGRANT

My Grandfather was one of the founders and Prophets of the Gospel of God Church of Africa, a small religious group founded in Zimbabwe in the 1900s. The church is known locally as Johane we Masowe.

My father's family emigrated from Zimbabwe (then Southern Rhodesia) to Botswana (Bechuanaland Protectorate) in the late 1940s. My grandfather, Hondzeri Boniface Mutero Chandiwana was one of the founders of the Gospel of God Church of Africa. He was also heir to the Chandiwana Royal family in Mahosu in Chivhu, Chikomba, Great Zimbabwe. My grandfather naturalised and became a Motswana after the independence of Botswana in 1966.

As a founder and prophet of the church, grandfather was selected to travel around Africa as a missionary, spreading the new-found gospel of God. The pilgrimage took him to Kenya, Zambia, Tanzania, Botswana and South Africa, in a religious quest. The descendants of the converts still live and worship in all of these countries today. Crucial to note, Moroka village is the centre for all the Bazezuru descendants

As my grandfather grew older, he decided to return home to Zimbabwe. He decided that on his way back home, he would pass through Bechuanaland. However, the war in Southern Rhodesia broke out faster than my grandfather had anticipated. This saw him settling permanently in Botswana. My grandfather did not attend any formal school, but he could read his bible in Shona, his native language.

This religious sect had beliefs and a way of life different than any other group in Moroka. My grandfather's religious sect allowed polygamy. Hence, he had three wives. My grandmother was the first wife. And my father was the first child.

In ancient African traditions, polygamy and observing God's patriarchal principles defined African society. It was about building empires, securing power and survival of the fittest. Children were a form of wealth and power; wives were a symbol of wealth. The more children and wives one had, the more powerful one was and the bigger the empire. Polygamy was a strategy. It was a strategy for men to show their virility and children who survived grew the family name and empire.

It was only after the colonial era that polygamy started to be shunned upon and eventually became less widespread. Colonialism, modernity, and colonial education were some of the causes of the decline of polygamy. My grandmother used to tell me that divorce was unheard of in the by-gone days. Big families meant there was better security, more food, and mutual support among relatives. Families stayed together and worked in harmony. Serious animosities were shunned upon as blood was perceived as being thicker than water.

Welcome His Royal Highness

His Royal Highness Prince Shadreck Mutero Chandiwana was born September 19th, 1939. My father was the first child in a family of six siblings. He had two sisters and three brothers. As a first born son, my father was second in line to throne after his father.

In Zimbabwe, we are of the Chandiwana Royal Family of Mahusvu, Chivhu. My grandfather was Chief of the tribe before converting to Christianity which did not allow him to mix royal duties with spiritual life. This meant that my father, as the first born child, missed the opportunity to be King because his father had chosen religion over royalty. My father tells me this was one of their arguments with his father and something he has never forgiven him for; neglecting his people and choosing religion. This was a very sensitive topic that my father would not give me a chance to interrogate further. However, he showed his rage and revenge by rebelling against his father's religious believes. He called it, civil disobedience.

The religious sect forbade formal education, so parents were not allowed to take their children to school or hospital. I observed a few deaths of children in the sect which today I believe, should there had been proper pre and post-natal care, those lives would have been saved. Pregnant mothers never saw a doctor. Home births were a norm and mandatory. These are a few of the tough rules that church members had to abide by.

My uncle Reneais Mutero speaks very candidly about my father, a person he had known all his life. They were very close friends and formed a lasting bond. I remember uncle Reneais coming to Moroka for his yearly visits to see his family. He also took this time to pay his respects to my grandfather, who was now deceased and was buried in Moroka Village. My grandfather passed on in the early 80's.

As I mentioned earlier, like other male congregants in church, the Prince of Mahusvu, my father was engaged in making basic household wares like pots and baskets, which were sold by the women-folk in the surrounding villages. Besides making these basic household wares, the men were also engaged in sundry casual jobs.

This was because according to the sect's philosophy, everyone had to be entrepreneurial. The saying goes, "You work for yourself, and God will multiply by several folds what you get at the end of the day". Admittedly, they worked hard but not smarter. The later generation congregants are still working hard with limited returns to sustain their basic family needs.

My mother met my father in Zimbabwe when she was working at a farm in the Mr Darwin area. When war broke out in the early 1970's in Zimbabwe, my mother feared she was a target because she was working for a white farmer. She then fled to Botswana with my father. It was there that they married and settled. They would later have five children; two boys and three girls and I am the second girl among the three. One of the boys died at birth as my mother gave birth at home.

Before meeting my father, my mother was married to her first husband and they were living in the village of Shengezi. She had four children from her first marriage. Once my mother fled to Botswana, her children were incorporated into my uncle's family, Sekuru Timothy Nduku. Today, my uncle still lives in Chitungwiza, Zimbabwe.

My mother always struggled with the idea of having left her children with their father who later abandoned them. Only to be rescued by her brother. This caused her so much guilt.

My paternal grandmother had a tremendous influence on my upbringing. She took care of us when my mother was away and later lived with us when she grew old. It was only fair that we would take care of our grandmother when she was frail.

My grandmother was very religious. I do not believe that she ever missed a church service. Her whole life revolved around church. This was normal for the First Lady to the founder of the church. I came to notice that women did not have any prominent role in the church except to be followers. The church is designed in such a way that men and boys sit at the front of the church and women and girls near the back. I do not remember my grandmother ever telling me anything to do with the administration of the church. She was a follower. This religion makes women followers.

LIFE IN THE CHURCH

The church carefully choreographs its members' lives. Religion is life and nothing else happens outside the church. This arrangement probably led me to nurse questions about my identity. I also asked myself how such a diverse community could embrace exclusion from public life. I wondered if the exclusion was a fundamental part of who we were.

A conversation with my grandmother:

Me: *Grandma, how come I cannot braid my hair like other girls in my class?*

Grandmother: *Only Gentiles (meaning people who did not live in the compound) can do that. We are pure. We can only wear white scarfs. This is what God wants from us.*

(I wondered if I was considered a gentile too since I seldom attended church).

Me: *But God made me with this hair? Why are you removing it?*

Grandmother: *God made you that way; God gave you a brain as well. Use it.*

This, for me, was a light-bulb moment. God had given me a brain, and I had to use it. I willed myself to be useful and relevant.

The village situation, however, compounded by the fact that these religious beliefs were not appreciated by other residents in Moroka village. Some of the practices were very unusual and I wondered how we were following them without question. These practices included not sending children to school and only marrying within the church. This meant that the church monopolized the most pivotal events in one's life. The decision concerning whom to marry and spend the rest of your life with, I believe, should be left for one to make. The monopolization of such decisions reinforced church control and power over its adherents.

There was so much pressure on the girl child when it came to marriage. From the day a girl child is born to the day she is married, her life is choreographed in preparation for her future husband. And every girl had to be married as a virgin. However, one of the many things that made me very uncomfortable was that most of these girls were given away to marriage very young. Most of them would be between the ages of fourteen and fifteen. When I fell pregnant at sixteen, it seemed normal because most of my peers had children. The only difference was that I was not married.

A girl's destiny was a carefully designed affair. On the first night of her wedding day, she would be tested. The ladies of the church, along with the aunties of the newlyweds, would determine where she slept. Tradition stipulated that they would make her bed for that first night.   This bedding included a crisp new white sheet bought by the groom's aunt.

In the morning, the bride and the groom were not expected to make their bed. The same group from the previous night would come in to check if the girl had passed the test. If there was no blood on the sheets, it was concluded that the girl was not a virgin. This was an embarrassment to the family and a cause for intimidation for the new bride.

I thought it was a cruel and shameful practice. This invasion of privacy left a taint on the bride for life. In a society that is primitive and ruled by these strict rules and pressures, this was extreme torture to the girls.

Grooms had it easier. Theirs was the burden of providing food for guests on their wedding day. This was still a shared task with the grooms' families yet the bride had to worry about the proceedings of that day as well as the virginal test to follow.

Poverty is among the worst forms of violence in this world. Like racism and prejudice, poverty is not natural. Every family in the compound with a girl child wished their daughter would marry a man who was richer than them. The girl would be their ticket out of poverty.

Although marriage in my tribe is one of the most respected institutions, one does not just marry their partner, they also marry their partner's family. Families were united through marriage. Sometimes marriages were arranged. Strange as it may sound, those marriages lasted. Even the polygamous marriages lasted until "death do us part". I do not know to what extent the national constitution allowed this, but it was allowed in the church.

Talking about sex with our parents was unheard of. It was taboo. If you had an affluent auntie, you could be lucky to get some of the small talks, but other than that, sex and love were never discussed. We could talk about it as cousins and friends in our play, but that was how far my knowledge of sex, love and marriage went. I learnt about the reproductive system in school and that was an exceptional experience as most girls from the church did not attend school. I always wondered if the young brides who were placed on the white sheets on their wedding nights had any idea of what was in store for them.

Apart from the white sheet practice, it was also mandatory to check if the bride's clitoris was long enough to satisfy the needs of the groom. Most of the girls in the compound pulled their clitorises to make them longer as an initiation into adulthood. The longer they were, the better the chances of satisfying one's husband. It was a form of pride when we used to bath together in the river and jostled to see who had longer ones among us.

Girls and women had to abide by a prescribed dress code; an all-white dress code from head to toe. Women had to wear head scarfs and were not allowed any makeup. The braiding of hair or anything artificial was therefore disallowed. However, for men and boys, any common styles of dressing were acceptable.

The other uncanny practice in this church was barring congregants from seeking medical attention from the hospital. Women gave birth at home. If a child was born in a hospital, the mother and the child had to be purified first before being allowed to attend church. I saw children die of measles and other opportunistic post-natal diseases that could have been treated at the hospital. This did not sit right with me. I recall my mother once telling me that my only brother had survived due to the medical attention he had received from the local hospital.

My brother Douglas was born prematurely at seven months. He had to stay in hospital till he was deemed healthy enough

31

to be discharged. Had my mother followed the strict instructions from the church, my brother would probably not be here today. I cannot imagine life without him. My brother is very special to me. He is the person I grew up idolising. To me, he is the kindest and funniest person I know. It grieves me to think that many have lost their siblings due to rigid church practices which forbade modern medical care.

This knowledge intensified my curiosity about our sect's way of life. I questioned everything about my grandfather's religious practices. However, by the time I was born, my father was no longer abiding by the strict principles of the church. But the shadow of the church still lingered into our way of life. Already my father had defied his faith and embarrassed his father, the founder of the church. We were now shunned upon as descendants of the prodigal son. This tremendous pressure to conform boggles me to this day.

The energy to continue looking for something different was provoked by what I saw around me. I had friends who braided their hair and those who did not wear white all year round. Friends who were allowed to love whomever they chose. In my deep quest for answers, I asked myself why we could not be the same as the other girls outside our sect. I sought to understand what had caused the restrictions in our lives.

To date, some questions linger on without sufficient or practical answers. However, I would speculate on some possible answers to these questions though I badly needed to be given credible answers. I have come to learn that if we are driven by fear and control, our choices can be self-defeating because there was something about being confined in the compound that seemed not right. One noticeable fact was how poor everyone was! Whether people accepted it or not, this was the reality on the ground. People seemed happy. They had roofs over their heads and never went to bed hungry.

By the time I reached fifth grade, I knew within me that there had to be more to life than what our sect allowed us to experience. I vowed I would do better with my life. I knew I wanted more than marriage and shelter. There had to be more to life and everything within me urged me to find out for myself.

IDENTITY CRISIS

Like most teenagers, I struggled with identity crisis. My parents did not make this easier either. As much as we were living in the compound, where people were supposed to be united and subscribing to the same set of rules, standards and protocols, my mother and father, who were direct relatives of the church's founder, were different. We did not dress like Bazezuru. We wore "normal" or "regular" clothes like everyone else in the village.

With all this confusion around me and no explanation given, other questions cropped up which did not allay things. Developing a sense of self or an identity is an essential part of every individual as we all mature. Not having a strong sense of self or struggling with identity issues, may lead to depression as a teenager.

Already my physical body was going through many changes which, when coupled with the identity issues I faced, made a great recipe for confusion and self-loathing. This is an experience I do not wish for anyone. It would take a while before I became comfortable with my own identity.

In fourth grade, as we prepared for national exams, I asked my mother to change my last name to Boniface, and my mother did not question it. This was my way of trying to evade the constant bullying that I suffered.

I spent most of my childhood outdoors. I had many friends from the Barolong side of the village and the Kalanga side. I had integrated very well into the Barolong who were more of the typical Tswana people in the village. As much as integration was easy for me, there was something about growing up a Zezuru that was different. I was not Tswana. I was not Kalanga. I was not "pure" Zezuru. So I repeatedly questioned who I was.

Not knowing and accepting the self is a torturous experience. This exposed me to bullying by my peers at school who always raised the issue of my identity. It seemed the rite of passage was for one to go through bullying and transcend it. I remember my first day at middle school as if it were yesterday. It was not unusual for students to miss school on the first day to avoid being hazed. The intimidation of new students was severe. The seniors would vandalise lockers, threaten violence and forcefully take away lunch from new students.

These are some of the unpleasant experiences that we had to deal with as new students. Had I known better, I would have fared better. It felt like we had been thrown into the belly of the beast and needed to survive. I had to adapt to my surroundings fast.

A specific incident that stands out from my schooling years concerns my last name. I began schooling a year earlier than most children. It had been a struggle to get me registered earlier but when the headmaster saw that I could spell my names, he was convinced that I could be admitted.

I was registered as Angelinah Hondzeri. Hondzeri was my grandfather's name and the school registrar knew our family. A year earlier, he had registered some children who had been adopted by my father under the same name. He therefore assumed I was Hondzeri too despite my birth registration certificate not showing this.

This surname became the reason I was bullied. None of my classmates could pronounce it well so they teased me about it. Around the time for fourth grade national examinations, I pleaded with my mother to have my surname changed. My father was, fortunately, using Boniface, my grandfather's second name as his surname. It was therefore reasonable that my surname was changed to Boniface to tally with my father's name. This is how I ended up with two English names. Despite it being easier for the other students to pronounce it, it however became one of the reasons for my identity crisis. I had no African name. I was neither Zimbabwean nor Motswana.

Where I come from, a name has a significant meaning. We have totems, and we have ethnic differences. Most names have meanings and significance and they are used to identify who you are. That is your people, your culture and your ancestry. The importance of this is engraved in us from the day we are born.

Now I stood as a young child losing my identity. My mother gave me an English name, and then I had an English last name, which I chose to use to avoid bullying. How was I to reconcile with this predicament? Was I supposed to adopt a Tswana name and change my birth certificate? That was a farfetched thought at my age.

As things stood, I had given up my birth name and it felt as though I had given up my birthright. My father, the church founder's son had defied the most basic of our sects and Bazezuru traditions. He had given all of us English names, my brother being named Douglas and my elder sister, Juliet. These foreign names bore no meaning or connection to our sect and culture.

My father had always been different, defying culture against all the odds. Shona, Kalanga and Tswana people always gave their children names that meant something in their cultures. For instance, my best friend at Primary school was Tolani, meaning "take". Then there was my neighbour, Kedisaletse "It

37

was all left for me." There was Dipuo which meant "gossip or too much of talking." Dimakatso meaning "shocking." Ditsietsi meaning "tribulation." Mlungisi meaning "the fixer."

As he grew older, my father had gradually softened up and probably began reconciling with his roots. He named my younger sister Lebogang. She is his last child and is the only one whose name means something to us. Her name means being thankful or being grateful. Lebo, as we call her, has no English name.

How come I never had an African name?

In my mind, by changing my strange last name, a new me would be born and most importantly, the bullying by my classmates would stop. To my surprise, the bullying persisted. My crisis worsened as I was stuck with an English name that meant nothing to my people and that did not stop the bullying. This felt like an unending nightmare. I had been determined to overcome bullying, but it clearly was not easy. A typical conversation with a bully went something like this:

Bully: *Hey face with a bone, come here. Hahaha!*

Me: *If that makes you sleep at night, so be it.*

Another Bully: *Hooondzeeeriii!!!*

Me: *As if that will boost your immune system.*

I developed a resistance mechanism by becoming isolated. But all the same, I felt battered by currents of intense resentment, anger and rage under a mask of indifference. I could feel I was strong inside so I vowed to block all negativity.

I also plunged into my studies and realised that most of these bullies were not smart. They may have been cleverer but they were certainly not smarter than me.

Between sixth and seventh grade, we had the same class teacher, Mr July. At elementary school, the same teacher taught all the subjects, Maths, English, Science, Social Studies, Setswana and Agriculture. The same students carried over together into the next class.

Primary school teachers were jacks of all trades which meant we had only one teacher per grade. The only time we had another teacher was when a teaching assistant from the national service took over for a while. Every year we could have two or three and most of the time, they would assist with the preparations for national examinations or cover for teachers who were away sick.

The bullying may have started way earlier, but it was in 6B and 7B when it worsened. However, Mr July was different.

His style of teaching was more creative and interesting than that of our previous teachers and I felt at home in his classroom. The main reason I liked Mr July was that he exposed the stupidity and dumbness of the bullies. He had a way of making us vulnerable, but it was more painful for the bullies. He would call students to solve either a Math problem or a spelling bee contest and the drama would unfold like this:

Mr July: Sithembile to the board. Dimakatso to the board. Akanyang to the board. Grace to the board. Nketleleng to the board. Angelinah to the board.

These students would all rise and line up at the board to solve the problem depending on the subject at hand.

My pleasure was seeing all the bullies getting the answers wrong and Mr July giving them corporal punishment. This, for me, was the best part of elementary school. It was painful. Months and at times the whole term would go by without me receiving any corporal punishment. I worked hard to avoid beatings. I would get all the Math problems and spellings correct.

At some point, Mr July stopped calling me to the board. Only the less focused students would be called out. Failing to solve arithmetic or algebra on time was deemed to be a reflection of laziness or of not having studied. This would, therefore, call for a beating. It was through this embarrassing and humiliating treatment that we got to know who was smart and who was not. I felt hurt by the bullies and I reasoned that this way, they felt hurt too. For me, their hurting was justice served.

As the bullies got humiliated, their bullying stopped and I began to work on my destiny. These bullies could not win. I began to reclaim my power, not only to transform myself but to transform my future.

What drove me was pain. The pain I had been feeling all that time when anyone said something demeaning. I vowed that something positive had to come out of this. I was determined to create my destiny. I refused to let the past determine my future.

Only I would change the situation at home. Being in school at that time meant grasping as much as I could. Life's challenges have a way of shaping us. The isolation and reservation ultimately drove me to study harder and it forged a desire to know and understand better. The desire to prove myself capable ironically came from being bullied. I realised that I had to prove myself and this instilled the work ethic and focus which has become second nature. It is no wonder I was to become the first in achieving many things in our family line. I may have lost my name but I did not lose the will and purpose of my life.

Identity and culture

Traditionally, kinship is two-pronged and can be established in terms of bloodline or totem, thereby integrating people within the extended family. There is a sense of identity that comes with a totem and it is the responsibility of each community to protect its symbolic animal.

The extended family is made up of an intricate kinship with parents, children, uncles, aunts, nieces, nephews, brothers and sisters, all regarding each other as closely related. Our culture is patrilineal, which means the father's side is more important than the mother's side. However, the maternal uncles take precedence in certain matters and occasions.

Totems are believed to protect people against taboos such as incest. People identify with totems to demonstrate close relationships with other people, animals and the environments they live in. And in a bigger sense, totems invoke a sense of belonging.

Among the Shona clans of Zimbabwe, the totem is seen as the prime signifier of culture and identity. For example, my clan is eland, "Mhofu ye Mukono" in Shona. It is the mandate of my clan to protect the eland from extinction by not eating it. You cannot eat your totem. It is taboo. There is also a sense of power that comes with a totem. It was one's responsibility not to harm that animal or plant but to rescue or care for it when in need. Totems were a form of protecting the environment, which I think was a traditional way of conservation. Bedtime stories while growing up were of tales about how men became heroes for rescuing their totem animals. To this end, totems are treasured and preserved for the community's good.

 As a norm or habit, when one meets someone for the first time, he or she tends to ask, "Whose child, are you?" And the answer is always your last name or the name of your clan. If you are from the same clan or have the same totem, by default you are related though you may not be blood relatives.

Over time, I have made many sisters, brothers and cousins from the clan name and totem. A sense of unity develops just by identifying with that animal even if you are not blood-related. The bigger the clan, the more power they have and the more powerful the name is. People have often used their clan names to command respect. African totems are a restoration of lost identities from colonialism. Establishing relationships this way has made it easier for a traveller or stranger to find social support.

Today, different totems can be identified among the Shona ethnic groups, and similar totems exist among South African groups, such as the Zulu, the Xhosa, the Ndebele, the Kalanga, the Herero and many more groups in Botswana, Zambia and Namibia.

Circumstances may influence who you are, but your destiny will live through. I was a dreamer, and that dream had to manifest itself. The passion within me drew me to diversity.

I came to realise that I was my father's daughter. You could not put my father in a box. He was a rebel. He rebelled against anything or anyone who would try to stereotype him. My father did not believe in fate, he believed in carving his own destiny. He believed you could be who you wanted to be no matter what the world threw at you. My father is my hero. This is the man who defied the odds when no one dared to challenge the status quo.

However, there was no way of distancing himself from the foundation that was already there. He was born into a royal clan that was governed by a strict set of beliefs.

REBELLING FROM THE SECT FOR A BETTER LIFE

My father did not want his children to be as poor and miserable as he had been. He was determined to cut the pattern.

He had left the church before I was born and joined a new church in the village called Saint Marks. It resembles the Methodist church. The main reason why he left his father's church was to ensure that he could freely send his children to school. Although my father did not attend formal school, he understood the importance of education. He was determined to cut the generational pattern of poverty. Poverty, both in knowledge and material terms.

My father was a ground-breaker, a pioneer and a trailblazer. He risked being isolated in an already extremely isolated society. He also risked being disowned by his father and his family were he to send his children to school but he did it anyway.

The first to go to school was my sister, followed closely by my brother and lastly by myself. We all went to Moroka Primary School.

As a result of this daring violation of the core beliefs of my society, my father was scorned, harassed and isolated by the elders of the church. Because we were still living in the compound and going to school, the church elders expected my father to follow the rules. If he did not, he had to leave the compound, the only home I had known all my life. It came to a point where the church became impatient with my father. He was excommunicated from the church and asked to leave the compound.

I had seen church leaders attempting to talk to my father to reconsider his decision and re-join the church. It was either that or he had to leave the compound but he was such a determined and strong person that for nearly a decade, they attempted and failed to get rid of him from the compound. He was a resistance movement by his own right and that fierceness made us proud of him.

I think my father thought it was his birth right. Since his father was the high priest and founding member, no one could chase him from the compound. He felt he was entitled to be there. He became aggressive and outrightly defied the elders who gradually felt themselves disarmed by this man's sheer rigidity.

But for one to really understand the reason for my father's intransigence, one must recognise that living in the compound was a sense of identity. It also meant we would be homeless if we were chased from our only place of residence. My father had too much pride to be embarrassed by the church his father had founded so he had to stand his ground in the face of a concerted challenge.

To leave the compound and get his own land, my father needed to go through the intricate process of applying for land. In communal lands like Moroka, one has to be invited or go around enquiring for available space. This was not an easy process as according to the statutes, all land belongs to the community and was given freely by the government. To think of losing a home that had been freely given to his clan by the government and having to start all over again was more than a nightmare.

Yet the pressure mounted as his people made it more uncomfortable for us to stay. He had to find a solution otherwise the animosity looming would destroy his family. The elders were determined to see him off.

I remember when I was in fourth grade, I found my mother fencing a farm on the path that was along the way to my school. I knew this route well as I used it often when going to and from school. I wondered what she was doing here and when I asked her, she made it clear that in time, this would be our new home. We were moving away from the compound. We had been chased out by our own people.

This was the first time I learnt not to trust anyone. How could the only people I thought were my family, chase us away? What wrong had my father done? What of us his children, what had we done? I felt like they were the ones who were wrong and callous. Everyone lived together in this big compound. It had seemed like one big family to me. Now I had lost the only family I had known since birth. I was now officially an outsider from my people because I could not relate to the terms of their religion.

Another question that bothered me in the aftermath of the rejection by the Bazezuru was, who was I since I was not identified as a Zezuru?

For the year that followed up to my fifth grade, I helped my mother to mould bricks to build a place we would call our new home. My father was a builder and he had to build the most beautiful huts for his family to live in. I was proud that at least I had assisted my parents to build this new home. I celebrated inside that I belonged there. I owned this place. I was safe. I still have many beautiful memories of this place which even today, I call home.

My father had chosen to settle a stone's throw from the compound so that he could take care of his the nailing mother. Five years later, the home came up beautifully. The roof leaked during the rainy season, and in autumn when the winds were strong, the roof would be torn away. When the roof leaked, I would take my mother's cans and place them where they could receive the water from the roof.

Some seasons the rain would be so strong that the cans would rapidly fill up and the floors would get flooded. If mother failed to make supper before the rains started pouring, we knew the night would be long.

I was witnessing this pattern every rainy season and it gave me the determination to change the situation at home. My ultimate dream against all odds was to build a nice house for my father. A house with no stones on the roof and which did not leak.

LIFE AFTER THE SECT

Life changed when my little sister was born ten years after me. All along it had been my elder brother Daggie, and I. My sister had already left at seventeen for the city. My brother has always been of few words and we never spent a lot of time together playing together because he was so timid. He felt more comfortable by himself and he pursued his own interests. The few times he would be around us is when mom was preparing dinner at night and he would sit around the fire. Even then, you would never hear my brother's voice.

When my sister arrived, I had a companion. I had something to look forward to when I returned home every day from school. The first time that I saw her, I loved her. I knew she in turn loved me. Despite our ten-year gap, I would take her everywhere. We played around the village and made friends together. Life was good. I would feel bad when I left her with my mother at home and went to school. When I came home every afternoon, she would be waiting for me at the gate.

Probably the best times I had growing up in school was at Moroka Primary School. The teachers were tough. We respected our teachers like they were gods. They had the best clothes and the best houses and spoke English. Teachers were the cream of the village. I adored them.

The first day of school in standard one was scary. I had not attended any school before. This would be my first encounter with school and other children from all over the village. The day before school, I had spent the afternoon practising how to write my name on the ground. It was January and it had rained the day before, which made playing on the ground fun. I had never held a pen or pencil before. I had seen my mother writing letters to her family but had never found the interest to learn what she was doing. I had no practice books or crayons but I had the ground and my fingers. This is how my sister taught me how to spell my name. I did not know the alphabet well but I would attempt to read.

The bell rang, and the students went pouring into the school. The excitement and chaos filled the air. My elder brother who was in the fifth grade had left me behind since he had to be there earlier than the first grade pupils. For some reason, the teacher who was to become my class teacher, recognised me because like other teachers, she knew my mother and she had seen me before. The teacher called me to the class.

We had to line up and wait for the daily scout drums to roll as we marched towards the centre of the school to the assembly area, class by class, from first to seventh grade. This was a ritual. Every morning, we marched like soldiers in a drill to the assembly area with the drums guiding our rhythm. This

51

went on for the seven years I was in elementary school. There was a drummer who sat under a tree wearing a Boy Scout tie, beating the drums to the marching tune till every class had made it to its assembly line. I have no idea how this guy never missed school. At the assembly, we would sing a song, listen to a bible verse or a bible story and recite the Lords' prayer then listen to announcements by the teachers.

It was at the assembly arena where we would gather at the end of each school term, and each class would announce the best ten students. The students would stand as their names were called out amid ululations from other students and teachers. This raised the bar for competitive students like me because I made sure I was in the best ten for the seven years I was in primary school. It happened from the first grade when I was position three out of the twenty-seven students. After that exhilarating feeling of triumph, I did not look back.

I also excelled in track and field events and sang in the school choir. We had regional competitions and our school would mostly scoop the first position. Time at this wonderful haven went by too fast.

What also made primary or elementary school special, was that my father built most of the buildings as a contractor. He was the builder of choice for the community. He would be around the school campus whenever there was an extension project going on. The seven years I was at the school, I saw my dad build almost six classrooms. I spent considerable time after school at the places where my father was putting up structures. When I knew where he would be working, I would go there after school.

As I grew older, I would help him sometimes by installing doors. We built houses for people in the village, yet our own home leaked. There were days I wished we could move into one of the houses we had built because they were far better than our own.

I came to realise later that my father was building all the homes on credit and people owed him money. People would come to him when they needed anything he could provide, and he would give them, including his labour. He would build houses for people, and they would owe him his money for years. He was a generous man and I know some people who still owe money to my deceased father to this day.

My father was a gifted builder but lacked the business acumen necessary to succeed in his trade and at his funeral, a few people came out and told the family that they owed him some money but they still did not pay up. I guess it made them feel better to just say it rather than to actually pay. If every one of his clients had paid my father his dues, he would have been among the wealthiest people in the village. But he never looked at it that way. He preferred peace rather than confrontation.

Hello Junior Middle School

Middle or junior school is probably one of the most difficult phases in a student's life. I had mixed fortunes. Firstly, because I had excelled in elementary school, I got into middle school with honours. I had proved to the bullies that bullying does not reduce the victim's performance. Ironically, most of the bullies had not fared well. I was among the best students along with my best friend, Maggie. We were the two girls out of the whole class who got A's. At the same time, my body had begun to change. The hormones were creeping in and I was a mess. My breasts became bigger and I gained weight. Luckily, I did not develop acne.

Ramoja Community Junior Secondary School is a secluded school in the middle of nowhere. Located between the three remote villages of Ramokgwebana, Moroka and Jacklas No.1, the school is an acronym of these three villages.

I would walk for eight kilometres with my school mates to and from Ramoja Community Junior Secondary School. It was a long route and it feels longer now yet back then, it was fun. I grew into a woman walking this distance. I became my own hero. Three years of junior school went by so fast. On my lucky day, I would get a lift to ease the strain. We did not have public transport to and from school, neither was there private transportation. The reluctance of private transportation to establish a route was probably due to the generally straitened circumstances of the villagers. Most people survived under $1 a day and could not afford to pay extra for transport. It would have been different if it was in the city. So we walked every day and the three years went by like a flash of light.

Lessons at the junior School started very early at 07:20 a.m, meaning I had to be up really early to make my 4 kms journey. The routine was the same each day: Alarm at 5am. Set fire to warm my bathing water then prepare myself mentally for the journey. It was an excruciating exercise. No wonder in the olden days, whoever started the fire first, became a chief. It takes a lot of skill and patience to get the fire going especially in the rainy season, with wet and uncooperative wood.

On the other hand, the agony was that the kitchen and the bedroom were separate rooms. This, together with the dark mornings at 5 am in Moroka, only worsened my discomfort. Because of my phobia for dark places, I would end up bathing in cold water even in winter.

My mother was pained to see me bathing in cold water so she decided to invest in our first ever paraffin stove. She did not think of the dangers of paraffin, and if she did, she still did not allow herself to be bothered. This was her way of alleviating a dire situation. Amazingly, this paraffin stove became my saving grace.

Before my mother's brilliant improvisation, I would spend hours during weekends and school holidays with my friendly neighbours in the woods, looking for a few dry branches for firewood. To avoid the gruelling mid-day sun, we would leave early in the morning before sunrise to return before the sun became intense. At that time in many towns and metropolitan areas, wood was widely used as the main source of fuel by low and middle-income families. Whenever I saw electric stoves during school summer breaks at my uncle's house in Harare, Zimbabwe, I would imagine a day when our home would be the same.

With the paraffin stove, it meant we had to get the paraffin, and it was not cheap. My mother discovered that there was a cheaper version of paraffin in neighbouring Zimbabwe. It became my responsibility every other weekend, to travel across the border to Plumtree, Zimbabwe to buy paraffin. I ended up becoming a supplier of paraffin in the village. I would get three 20litres of cheap paraffin from Zimbabwe, two for my personal use and one for sale. This kept me going until middle school was over. It was not legal to bring paraffin on public transport, but I made friends along the way who were sympathetic to my situation. I was young and innocent yet exuded a level of responsibility that touched some people, and they helped me to smuggle my paraffin.

My favourite subject in junior school was Home Economics. We had a whole laboratory that had cooking utensils for practicals. I loved the laboratory because of the fridge and the four burner gas stove with the oven. Not many homes had that kind of stove. We did not have it at home. We used firewood and the closest I had been to a stove was my mother's one burner paraffin stand stove. My mother had warned me a couple of times about the dangers of using the paraffin stove in case I wanted to use it in her absence. She always told me I had to handle paraffin with extreme care, as it is poisonous and can cause severe illness, or even death if digested.

Also, paraffin stoves when knocked over, can explode and cause serious injuries and fires. In addition, depending on the type of paraffin used, the smoke and smell from the stove are extremely dangerous. Listening to her narration of all these hazards made me wonder, "How about the four-burner in school?" I had learnt to cook on that burner stove at school under the watchful eyes of the teachers.

I grew so fast and I was smart. I was clean and I was the class monitor. This leadership role was taken very seriously in junior school especially since my class was a class of elites and honour rolls.

I was still a bit shy, but when I needed to, I would not let boys bully me. I joined the athletics club and the chess club mainly because these clubs would travel every weekend. I had an opportunity to travel to many places in the country. Our Mathematics teacher was the coordinator of the chess club. He was very funny, charismatic and caring. I remember at times when I did not have any pocket money for trips, he would go out of his way to buy lunch and snacks, not only for me but for everyone. Because of this, no one was left out.

The girls' chess team was not as strong as the boys', but we did our best in a game that was not popular with girls at that time. I had been to Gaborone, the capital city, a few times, which was a great privilege, but every time I went with the chess club, it was fun. We were a small group and we were very close to each other. The conversations we had revolved around boys and our teachers. On some trips, we would be driven by our Principal in our school van.

Our Principal was a British expatriate named Mr Elson. He was a tall, well-built white man who was a bit intimidating but very calm and humble. He would usually break into a cold and grim smile which I failed to understand. Mr Elson did not speak any Setswana, which meant we had to communicate with him in English.

The difference when it came to communication with other staff members was that at Primary school, we could speak with our teachers in any of the local dialects as long as the teacher understood. Although all subjects were in English except the language classes, the teachers were lenient enough should English fail us. The story was different with Mr Nelson who only spoke English. That was my first challenge, to improve my English and do it with speed. I think it was a common concern for other students, though we did not talk about it.

Most of the times, I never understood him because of his British accent, but he was such a pleasure to be around and a great principal as well.

The structure of classes at Ramoja Middle School was different from what we were used to at the Primary School. There were more subjects, more teachers and more classes that were specialised. The school had made it so competitive such that "A" students from the three different elementary schools were in one class. The Bs, together and the rest,

59

made up the remaining classes. I was coming from Moroka Primary School as an A student so I had the responsibility of making my village proud as well as to prove to the bullies that I was still excelling.

Our class had all the privileges. In everything we did, we would come out first place. The school was not as big and scary as I had expected. It was manageable.

We had to keep the school clean and we had to do the cleaning ourselves. We did not have janitors. We would do a general cleaning competition every fourth Friday that would always earn us prizes. The teachers on duty would award points to all the twelve classes. The class which got the highest mark received a prize that would be shared on the following Monday.. It was always cookies, the choice assorted brand. We loved those cookies and looked forward to winning as a class so that we would enjoy them again.

My class won most of the time during my period at Ramoja. My leadership skills began there as a class monitor. I would be the first to start cleaning and the last to leave the classroom. We would choose boys who would stay behind until the teachers came by to ensure that no one would throw dirt into our class and make us lose points. This was my winning strategy.

The class monitor was also responsible for serving lunch. We had two meals a day at school. For some, probably it was the only hot meal they had. I would serve all my classmates and make sure that there was a roster for cleaning the dishes. This was a challenging responsibility as most of my classmates were older than me.

I never missed a day of school unless I was sick, which was rare. The motivation was the food. Wednesday was my favourite. We had rice, fried chicken and coleslaw salad then. Wednesday was like Christmas for me. Therefore, the school was the place to be, no matter the circumstances.

I remember during very cold winters and rainy autumns, I would brace for the 4km journey knowing that I would have hot meals for breakfast and lunch. They say all you need is love, but I say all I needed was food. To this day, some of the best chicken and rice I have had was at that school.

I still excelled academically though some new subjects were a challenge, particularly Agriculture and Setswana Literature. With Agriculture, it was the gardening and the practicals that got me. I loved Social Studies mainly because of the teacher, Mr SB. He was a giant, gentle, charismatic guy and indeed cared that all students did well.

In one of my school reports, Mr SB noted that I was intelligent but too reserved. I was quiet, calm and shy. I knew deep in me there was a hero to be unleashed. If I noticed a club that embarked on trips, I would join it so that I could travel because it was free. I enjoyed my friendship with my classmates and other students in the school. Even though I live abroad now, I am still in touch with the Ramoja class of 1998 through social media platforms.

My goal of going into high school was to get all the best grades so that I could get into college. The only prestigious college in the country is the University of Botswana (UB). I had seen the University of Botswana years before when we visited the city on school chess trips.

I had seen the red brick fence and the nice tree-lined roads which surrounded the university. I always imagined how it was like inside. I did not know anyone at that time who was at UB so that I could visit but I wanted to go in and see things for myself. I only wished to set my foot in there in case I never made it. It was on a day in August when I once again beheld the campus and it looked really quiet and deserted. I came to learn that every August, UB would be on semester break. That picture stuck in my mind and I vowed that one day I would make it there.

An opportunity would arise for me a few years later.

First, I had to do high school. I started thinking about which high school would increase my chances of getting into college. Most of these schools had high pass rates including St Joseph's College, Mater Spei College, Moeding College, to mention a few. These were the ivy leagues of high schools in Botswana. I wanted to attend one of those. It was not as easy as I had imagined. Public schools in Botswana like in other countries, are zoned and transfers are very strict. What it meant was that I was going to be admitted in my zoned high school, Masunga Senior School. Masunga school then had a low pass rate and this did not inspire confidence. So as soon as the results were out, I began my campaign to get into Mater Spei College.

First, I needed to convince my friend Maggie, that we could do it together. We made a pact to convince our parents that we were Mater Spei material, not Masunga. This was the easy part. However, the difficult part was to convince the regional office at the Ministry of Education and Mater Spei College, why we wanted to enrol there. We did not have much of a valid reason except that we wanted to increase our chances of getting into college. Whilst this sounded good enough for us, we wondered if it would suffice for the regional board.

After collecting our transcripts from Ramoja CJSS, we boarded an early morning bus to Francistown for Mater Spei, with no return fare. We planned to ambush my sister while she was at work and tell her we were stuck and we needed to get back home. We had not told her about our plan but we expected her to assist us with the return fare anyway.

Maggie and I arrived in Francistown just before 10 am and headed straight to the school. It was a ten to fifteen minutes' walk from the bus rank. We got there and asked for the Administrator.

Administrator. *"Do you have an appointment."*

Us: *"No ma'am".*

Administrator. *"What brings you here, my children?"*

Me: *"We have been admitted at Masunga Senior, and we would like you to consider us here at Mater Spei."*

Administrator. *(With a sarcastic smile) "Who told you, that you could do that? Things do not work like that. We can't just admit you here".*

Me: *"Ma'am, we passed very well. We have straight A's."*

Administrator: "Congratulations my kids. But that's not the procedure. You need a special reason for you to get a transfer from Masunga to Mater Spei. The transfer has to be sent to us by Masunga Senior School. Sorry, we can't help you."

END OF STORY

We stood there, looking as miserable as ever, seeking all the sympathy. It did not work. We never made it into Mater Spei. In my mind, there was my future fleeing. I thought I would never see the gate of the University of Botswana. This was supposed to be my ticket to a great future and it was slipping away. I was hurt but later, I was proud that at least, we had tried.

Three weeks later, Maggie and I packed our bags for Masunga, and we were freshmen at our new school.

Life Not as Planned

I was on my way to prosperity. None of my family members had graduated from junior school. Both my sister and brother had quit school at seventh grade.

Amazingly, high school started smoothly. Masunga Senior High School was a boarding school, so I lived on campus. We were six of us in a dorm and I had a nice small bed for myself. There was very little privacy, but it was a great adventure though it would last only for one term.

By April of the first term, I discovered I was pregnant and I was devastated. I dropped out of school. Now here I was, my hope to get my father a house with no stones on the roof, all gone! It was back to square one. I was a disgrace to the family. My mother was not happy and I could not face my father.

One day I went for a weekend out of school boarding facilities and never came back. I was on the run. I could not stay with my mother and father due to my mother's rage. I chose my sister's place in the city. Every day I cried myself to sleep. My father had got himself excommunicated from his community so that I could go to school and now this shame!

When my son was born on October 6th, 1999, it was the best day of my life. He was the most beautiful thing I had ever seen. He looked exactly like me although he had his father's physique. He was quiet, gentle and handsome and his smile could melt a block of ice. I was now a parent. I had a responsibility. One day I was a thriving teen in school, the next I was a mother! All my dreams had been shattered.

We were poor. We had nothing. How could I sabotage my only hope of getting an education? Maybe the community was right after all, education was not meant for people like me. I was born in a religious sect that had no respect for formal education, with zero percent literacy. What if this was my destiny? What if...? These thoughts kept coming, the doubts, the shame, the fear and the embarrassment.

I took my son home. Each day that passed by, I felt like I was drifting further and further away from my dreams. I was hopeless. I was angry. I was devastated, afraid and ashamed of facing the community. The community that had once seen me as someone heading somewhere. Yet here I was, heading nowhere.

Growing up in church, sex before marriage was a sin. I had sinned. I was a disgrace. It was hard to fathom. If this did not make me stronger, nothing would. I was a good child growing up. I was intelligent, calm and beautiful. I was supposed to be perfect, without blemish. Society already had high expectations of me.

However, I learnt quickly that good people do make mistakes. No one is immune to mistakes. Each day that passed by seemed like a year had gone past. I was in the village with my mother. There was no TV, no internet, just a battery-operated stereo that belonged to my brother. It was lonely, but I found love and peace in my son. I learnt how to love myself through the love that I saw in my son's eyes. Sometimes it's the little ones who will show you what it means to be alive. My son drew me back to me. This is why it was exceedingly difficult for me to leave him at home when I had to go back to school.

When they don't believe you

Abuse comes in many forms, not all of which are physical. When someone repeatedly uses words to demean and frighten you, this can take a toll on you.

I have always felt it in my gut when something is not right. The name-calling and personal attacks were demeaning and horrifying. I grew up in a society that tolerated fondling and flirting but I was convinced that it did not matter how much society condoned and practised it, a wrong is a wrong. The difficulty, however, comes when one attempts to speak up and society does all it can to silence you and choose not to believe you.

It hurts even more when the disbelief comes from the people you love and look up to. When society puts a sticker on you based on perception, it hurts.

I suffered a lot of verbal and emotional abuse from a family member who was supposed to be my protector. The fondling was degrading, the flirting was annoying, yet the person who was supposed to protect me was silent. I also kept quiet because I was scared, I would destroy the relationship they had. I did not want to be blamed for that. For many years it affected me. No matter how hard I tried to put up a brave front, I was hurting inside.

For a long time, I shut out everything that was happening to and around me. I thought I deserved every painful thing that came my way. I stopped believing in God because nothing made sense. I continuously wondered why this had happened to me. Was God punishing me for my sins?

I became very reserved and hardly ever expressed my hurt and shame. The truth is, I did not believe I was worthy of love. I hated myself. For many years I laughed it off when boys I dated asked me why I never said I loved them.   That monster had stolen my ability to love and be loved. This monster smoked marijuana all day and all that came out of his mouth were hurtful words.

The systematic cultural abuse of girls and women especially in rural areas is overwhelming. It is very easy for an older man to abuse young girls and hide behind the excuse of culture. Cultural norms that see women as sexual objects imperil women and young girls. They become easy targets to the sexual whims of men.

However, the irony is that to a certain extent, this also happens to boys. Where I come from, a young boy's private parts, when they are between the ages of zero to six, are seen as cigars. As a way of playing with the boys, who naturally roam around the compounds half-naked, the elderly women would sniff the boys' privates pretending to "smoke" them.

This practice is done jokingly and playfully therefore it is perfectly-regarded as normal.

Older men, on their part, would call young girls, "nkadzana" meaning 'my little wife'. This type of talk predisposes young girls to sexual indulgence and reinforces their conventional roles as wives and mothers.

After giving birth to my son, I could not go back to my former school because the principal there refused to re-admit me. I moved to the city so I could finish high school. This meant staying with relatives in unbearable conditions. The family member who had become my rock had a history of verbal abuse. His flirting and awkward conversations always left me speechless. At first, I thought his behaviour was alcohol-driven because he was always smoking weed and drinking alcohol until I realised that there was no excuse for committing a wrong and blaming it on alcohol.

Already I was a woman and I had a child. I knew what it was to sleep with a man and I was disgusted with the flirting and cheap romantic talk that kept coming. My one-night stand had led to a child and now as I was trying to get my life back, I had to deal with this. So I trusted no one when it came to any flirting.

The only person I decided to confide to about my ordeal was my church deacon. I knew no one else would believe me, and nothing would be done about it. I feared that since flirting was a cultural norm, I could even be vilified but I decided to try my luck anyway.

That deacon happened to be a police officer. I walked to his house in the middle of the day under a blazing sun. He was not at home, but his wife was there. She was surprised to see me. She later told me that the day I had showed up at her door, I looked like my soul had been removed from my body. I was walking and moving, but I was empty. Until today, I do agree with her perception of me that day.

I stood there quietly as I waited for the deacon to come home. The wife looked nervous because I had never before come to their house. She must have been wondering what exactly had happened that had brought me to their door in the heat of a dry summer.

She offered me a drink and tried to draw me into the conversation, but I had no interest in chit chat. I was as nervous as she was and this only made the atmosphere heavier. It was like both of us were locked in a prison we could not escape from and my wish for the Deacon's arrival was becoming more desperate with each passing second.

The deacon finally arrived after what seemed to be a lifetime. I sobbed as I told him my story. I was tired of being hurt. I was no longer going to allow this man to continue to abuse me. Everything poured from my heart like a flooding stream and as soon as I had finished talking, I felt like a heavy burden had been lifted off my shoulders. It was now up to him to take action. The confusion which played on his face showed that he was wondering what to do with this information.

As the deacon, he had an obligation to do something, to intervene in a way that would help a desperate soul. He also had a legal obligation as a police officer. After quiet introspection, the deacon and his wife proposed that I spend the night at their place to get ample time to come up with a credible course of action. I later learned that the Deacon did not know what my family would think about him accommodating me and he had to play his cards carefully as this was a delicate affair.

For me, however, it was a relief. For the first time in a very long time, I felt empowered. I felt good about myself for making that decision to speak to someone. However, at the back of my mind, I still dreaded having to face my family. Just as the deacon feared what my family would think, I was scared too.

I had left home with nothing and the following day was a school day. I needed my uniform for school. We decided that I would go to go pick up my uniform and other essential items. The deacon and his wife escorted me, although they did not enter the house. I was extremely disappointed as no one had bothered to look for me. Everything was normal just like nothing had happened at all.

I picked up my uniforms, and no one said a word to me or even asked me where I was going. They let me go. The tension was tangible, one could almost touch it but I did not collapse, I held onto the minute remnants of balance that remained in me so that I was able to appear less than vulnerable.

I had not slept the previous night and I felt tired especially with the sense of guilt that threatened to overwhelm my apparent composure any minute. I did not know what I had done to deserve such cold treatment but something told me that I had to hold my own as I had come to the point of no return.

Mrs Goitsemang, the Guidance and Counselling teacher, was a very approachable and calm lady. As I walked up to her office, I was trembling. She knew part of my story as a teenage mother, but she did not know how deep it was and what I was about to divulge to her.

As I told my story, Mrs Goitsemang cried with me. She immediately asked me what I wished to be done. My wish was to have a roof over my head and proceed with my education, I told her. I did not want to be homeless. She was very understanding and her empathy was absolute, so she pledged to support me in any way she could.

The wonderful thing about Botswana is that homelessness is not condoned. Friends and family should accommodate one of theirs. Mrs Goitsemang asked me if I had any other relatives in town where I could stay. It was a hard decision to make because I did not want to cause any strain between my family and our relatives, some of whom resented me already. However, my aunt, who was a distant relative, later took me in even though her house was already crowded.

I chose her because she was not a close relative. I was protecting my mother and father from the shame and resentment that they were already facing from other close family members because of my actions.

So after the incident, I moved out to live with Aunty Mai Isaac. My aunt has a good heart and a different way of looking at things. She gave me the benefit of doubt. She probably had her own opinions, but she never displayed any malice. Aunt had informally adopted my other cousins, with whom I had the pleasure of sharing the six by six feet bedroom, together with her daughter Abi. So it was four girls in that small space. We had a single twin bed, which meant some of us had to sleep on the floor. I could not care less about where I was sleeping. I was just happy to have a roof over my head.

I have heard too many stories about sexual assault against women and girls. Of all the stories I have heard, there is none that is better. Each story is different, experienced differently and must be treated differently. I did not want to be a statistic.

For a long time, this traumatic experience had affected my relationships. Even with friends, I could not be affectionate. I struggled to trust anyone and it has taken great courage for me to open up with warmth towards family and friends alike. To this day, I still fail to trust men as I feel that the ones who were supposed to protect me from the harsh realities of the world, failed to do so and instead judged me for standing up against one of their own.

This experience made me to be protective of my feelings. I suffered a lot in the effort to please a society that had relegated me as a miscreant. I knew, even then, that some of the things I did were not part of my morals but I still did them. For a long time, I could not face myself as I did not like the reflection I saw in the mirror. I even wished I was someone else so I preferred wearing other people's clothes, not my own, but something had to change. I could not continue like this because I was heading nowhere else but towards the precipice.

I started reading a lot of inspirational books. I went to church and volunteered to be a Sunday school teacher. Seeing those little children every Sunday, inspired me to be a better person. They looked up to me. I needed to pay attention to every step I took knowing that someone was looking up to me.

It was when some of the girls at Sunday school started coming to me for advice that I realised I was providing inspiration to others. I actually saw some of these girls making the same mistakes that I had made. It was like watching a movie of my life. I saw myself in these girls' shoes and it hurt me so much.

I then decided that my purpose in life was to make sure no other girl I knew, would go through what I had gone through. My life story is my greatest tool. It has provided me with the tools to look at life from many angles.

The Sunday School children at the Old Apostolic Church in Gaborone, saved my soul. I am grateful to them, as well as my Guidance and Counselling teacher and my Deacon who bothered to listen to me. They helped me find myself amidst all my confusion and gave me my voice back.

I knew I could not be empathetic to their stories and be true to them if I was not authentic to myself. It would be so hard for me to listen and be helpful to these children if I was not true to myself. The children showed me that I did not have to be perfect. I needed to be myself at all times. I was no longer afraid. I knew then that I was worthy just as I was.

OVERCOMING

Teenage pregnancy is a crisis for the teen mom, teen dad and their families. The odds are even greater for the teen mother who has to face the inevitable reaction of society. This experience taught me that having a support system makes a huge difference. A support system may come in the form of family, friends, church and the school community. As a community, it is necessary to encourage the teenage mother to discuss the options about how she plans to move forward. I also believe that the father of the child and his family should be part of the support system for the new parent. More importantly, the teenage mother should be encouraged to seek help from the health care provider. Talking to a psychologist or social worker also might be helpful.

Remember, love, kindness and support go a long way. Practise empathy every day. Listening without being quick to judge, that's all she needs to boost her self-confidence and get back on track.

As someone who now understood the significance of education, my heart throbbed with pain at the thought that I might never be able to cut the general curse of poverty in my family. Technically, my life had changed forever when my son was born. Life would never be the same again for me. I was practically a child with a baby. I wondered how God could have allowed this to happen.

My sister was already providing for me while I was pregnant. There was already friction and tension between the families of my baby's father and mine. We were both young. It had become a norm in our society that boys did not take responsibility for making girls pregnant. It became the sole burden of the girl and her family. The system also penalises the girls by expelling them from school whilst the boy is left scot-free.

When it was time to go back to school, my parents played a crucial part. My mother nursed my three-month-old son and my father became the provider until I had finished high school. My father had agreed to support my son but on the condition that I returned to school and later pursue a high school diploma. It was a clear-cut deal. If it were not for them, I would not have survived this monumental challenge.

Part 2

THE SACRED DREAM

One thing I knew for certain from an early age, is that I would never become the woman my grandfather's sect prescribed. I knew I would not get married early in life and become content with selling home-made wares. I wanted better in life. I wanted to be able to help my mother and enjoy a fulfilling life.

One spring night, in 1993, I had a dream. I recall this year very well because that was the year my sister was born. The dream was so clear that I had to tell someone. So I told my elder sister. In the dream, I was on a plane. I was wearing a white suit, flying above the clouds to a destination unknown to me. The only thing I knew about planes is that they go overseas. I had never been on one before and never thought I could be on one except in my dreams.

Incidentally, we had started learning about international organisations in fourth grade. The only ones I could understand well were the World Health Organisation (W.H.O) and the Food and Agriculture Organisation (F.A.O). In my mind, they sounded benevolent, busy and prestigious. I wanted to work overseas for the WHO. I despised farming and getting dirty so naturally, I gravitated towards WHO.

In my dream, the plane never landed and I woke up while we were still in mid-air.

Years later, I visited my elder sister who was living in Bulawayo, Zimbabwe. She was a very spiritual woman. It was easy to dismiss her as crazy but she was highly spiritual. She believed in prophecies and she took me to one of her spiritual guides. The aim was to look into my future. This prophet said a lot of things most of which I have forgotten. What I do remember was the tingly sensation down my spine when he mentioned that he had seen me in a plane, going somewhere far. I had looked at this man and thought he was crazy. My prospects seemed very dim and it was hard to imagine such a lofty thing could ever manifest in my life. Yet somehow it stuck in my mind. During the whole process of the "physic" reading or the prophecy, I wanted to leave the room, but I respected my sister enough to not want to cause a scene. Inwardly, I laughed at the absurdity of it all.

I had prayed to God for my life to be different and fulfilling. That I would not allow fear to paralyse my ambitions and my life would be an inspiration to others. But none of my prayers had been about going to a faraway place on a plane.

VISION AND MANIFESTATION
OF ENERGY

It is difficult to predict the future, but we can always work for a future we desire. I am grateful to the universe for aligning its energy with mine, which ultimately made my dream to become true. This is most significant for me since this has come to be, despite not having had a clear-cut framework or model from which to conjure inspiration or direction.

With very few role models to look up to, I had nothing to align my vision. Naturally, I looked for fulfilment from women around me. I idolised my teachers, the librarian at my high school, the nurses at the clinic and any such woman who looked like she had a grip on her life. Maybe one day, I thought, I would walk in their shoes and be the one with nice polished nails and manicured toes.

I loved the nurses' uniforms, from the white gowns to the shoes, as they walked confidently around the clinic. Whenever I would go to the clinic, I would gaze with awe at them and whisper to myself, "This is it. This is the life I want." Their confidence and the way they carried themselves with dignity and high regard, drew me to them. When I felt daring, I would think that maybe in time, I would be able to build my father a house...

There was no blueprint for me to move past my teenage pregnancy. It was more challenging because at every turn, there was a new set of obstacles and difficulties. In hindsight, I am grateful for each obstacle because they became the milestones through which I learnt lessons and became me. Each new challenge provided lessons that allowed me to grow and made me a better person. Every obstacle awakened a new me.

I am grateful for these lessons from Pastor Joel Osteen.

We carry so much baggage and often have to keep up appearances, so we are not judged as weak.

All the obstacles that I overcame helped me to acknowledge my insecurities, inadequacies and shortcomings so I accepted that I needed help. I learnt to be bold enough to speak up and ask for help. That way, I was able to get the assistance I needed and to do the work necessary to move forward.

It is my constant prayer that everyone, whilst on their journey, finds the right angels to assist them with the challenges they might be going through. And more importantly, to get the courage to seek and ask for help. There is no situation that is too big to be resolved. Whatever you may be going through today, seek help.

Pastor Joel Osteen is one of my greatest teachers of all time. One day I listened to his sermon on television. He mentioned that God's vision always comes with a provision. There is no way that God can put something on our table that we cannot handle. God always provides a way. God always answers. It may not be the answer we expected, it may be delayed but delay doesn't mean denied.

This was my light-bulb moment. This was the first time that I had heard someone talking of vision and provision. I am not a person to create a vision, write journals or diarize. My vision is in my head. I thought I could always remember important things if they were meant for me. My vision was in me, walking with me, sleeping with me and alive in me. I just needed to make it a reality. I thought I had figured out how to achieve it and that was through education as prescribed by my father. I figured education would have a way of sorting out my future and that I would somehow acquire my happily-ever-after from it. Beyond this, there was nothing else.

After that sermon by Pastor Joel Osteen, I began reading more about vision and provision. I chose to read verses in the Bible about vision. My favourite to date reads: "Where there is no vision, the people perish". This confirmed to me that I needed to create a vision for myself and my life and be ready to do the work for that vision to manifest in my life. I now sleep with a pen and notepad next to my bed to write all my thoughts and dreams.

The following was a lesson I learnt from one of my high school teachers at one of the assembly meetings:

Mr Mazviduma was a very charismatic man with a great sense of humour. Most of us knew him as a guy whom we could hang out with in the school corridors and have a good laugh. Unlike other scary teachers, he was very approachable, and we never took him seriously. However, on this particular day, Mr Mazviduma came with a huge surprise we had not seen coming.

He had a very compelling message that resonated with most of us. That day, you could feel a pin drop at the assembly area when he spoke. He mentioned how he had been thinking about this message for a while, especially as he has seen some us drifting away from the real purpose of why we were in school. He reminded us that the only person who truly knew and understood our situation back at home was us. It would, therefore, be up to us to see how best we could change the realities at home.

He further emphasised that change begins with the individual and that everyone had the power to become what they aspired to be in life.

This message has stuck with me, probably because for some weird reason that day, I happened to be the one leading assembly and I was in front of the school. I thought this teacher was speaking directly to me. The message was clear. The only way for us to achieve the change we wanted to see with our families was to change our pace and focus. If not, whatever we loathed about our current reality would remain as it was. This hit a nerve and got me thinking.

I felt the pain of growing up poor as I pictured our home. I felt the pain of bringing shame and disappointment to my family when I had become a teenage mother. The shame, the guilt, the hurt, all surfaced once again. Something had to change, and it was up to me and it was meant to be me.

I excelled in academics. I assumed leadership roles in the school. I set goals and set my bar high. I had to persevere. Whether it was examination papers or Sunday school teaching. Every class in college and everything else I have encountered in life and conquered has been motivated by that message from my high school teacher. Somehow, that made me believe I had the power to change the trajectory of my life. I was empowered. I am of the opinion that once one is decided on something, the universe conspires to help.

I had a vision. I believed the provision would come. I just needed to align my energy with that of the universe and make fireworks.

Where there is a vision, there is a provision.

CHRISTMAS IN THE VILLAGE

Anyone who knows me can attest to my love for Christmas. The Christmas season in Moroka made the whole village come to life. We did not have gigantic Christmas trees, exquisite decorations and lights, or candy, but we had each other. Santa Claus was a phenomenon we would hear about but we never dreamt that he would show up in our village. Besides, because Santa is white, there was little hope for any white person arriving in Moroka on any day, let alone on Christmas day.

In Europe, people get busy buying Christmas presents. Where I come from, we get busy queuing at supermarkets, buying food for Christmas. Christmas was the opportunity to eat good food. Food that you do not get to eat at other times of the year. Envision Fourth of July in the United States or thanksgiving combined in a day. This is Christmas in Moroka.

What also makes the village vibrant during the Christmas season is football. The local teams compete in local tournaments to be champions of the village. People came from the city to watch and cheer on their favourite players. The two favourites were Moroka Swallows and Young Stars.

For the longest time, these were the only teams in the village. Today there are about fifteen teams.

Football or soccer in the US and Canada is home to some of the sport's most passionate fans. From constant singing, fireworks, floods of flares to sambaing, hard-core fans have their incredible ways of supporting their teams. This is not different in Moroka. Football here is associated with passion, emotion, excitement and dedication.

The extreme emotional tone at football games characterises all aspects of discussions amongst village fans with some referring to the 'pure joy' and exhilaration of being at these games. The intensity of the experience actually makes some cry at these football matches. These could be tears of joy but sometimes, those of despair. Football provides for many fans an opportunity to let themselves go emotionally and to release the frustrations of everyday life. Football unites people in a bond of passion and excitement.

It was at these games that as children, we got the opportunity to parade and show off our new clothes and shoes. Those who got new clothes would be regarded as coming from affluent families that could afford extra luxuries. For the rest of us, food, especially Christmas food, was enough to cause delight. Our definition of Christmas was therefore good food, feasting with neighbours, wearing decent clothes and football. One could say, yes, we got presents from Santa in the form of clothes to wear to the football matches and show off to your friends. The years I didn't have clothes, I wouldn't go for the football matches to avoid the embarrassment.

A typical Christmas meal was chicken, rice, assorted salads, and dessert. You would get soda if there were extras. If there were no salads, then mayonnaise and tomato sauce (ketchup) would do the work. We hardly got the salads and any extras but we still managed to make it work.

One can then wonder what the meal on a normal day was like. It does not mean that there was no rice or chicken. It was only that on Christmas day, there were bountiful rations of this delicacy.

Our favourite meal in Botswana is beef and *pap* (boiled maize meal). *Pap* is the starch or carbohydrate made from maize meal and looks like mashed potatoes. This is usually accompanied by any choice of vegetables, like pumpkin leaves, bean leaves or even kale or spinach. The staple food in Botswana is sorghum.

Today, living abroad, I cannot go for a week without eating this special dish. My children, who have also lived most of their childhood abroad, have come to appreciate my African food. My happy place is when I cook food from home and share it with people from other parts of the world. It gives me so much joy sharing a part of my Africa with others.

In recent times, whilst in New York City, the school at which my daughter learns, hosted an international dinner fundraiser. I offered to cook dishes from Botswana. I made six dishes and had people requesting for second and third servings. My stand was opposite the Chinese stand. At first, I was nervous knowing how people love Chinese food. New Yorkers love Chinese food, and having them across the aisle was a bit intimidating. I thought people would flock to the Chinese food stand, ignoring mine. I was wrong. Food unites people. It turned out that people loved Botswana food. The joy I experienced while explaining where the food came from, and the dish itself, was so fulfilling. I could do this any day. One can never go wrong with feeding people good food. I guess for me, that's the joy that came with Christmas as I was growing up. Good food and happy people are what defined Christmas.

The icing on the cake for Christmas in the village would be if my team, Moroka Swallows, won the championship.

SWEET AND SOUR JANUARY

January is my birth month, hence, it is a very special month to me. While it is special to me, it is also a very sad month as my father passed on six days before my eighteenth birthday. Ever since it has been hard for me to celebrate my birthday.

Dealing or coping with the loss of a loved one is one of the biggest challenges anyone can go through.

When I lost my father, I lost a part of me. However, I chastised myself to remain focused on the good he would have wanted to see me achieve. I reasoned that this was yet another chapter of my life of which I had the choice to remain stuck on or move from. I was sure my father would have been very sad to see me stuck. I had to move on, not only for me but for him. I had to graduate from college and be the person he would have wished me to be. Though dead, my father was still my inspiration. On my toughest days, I would wake up and wonder what it is my father would have done had he been in a similar situation.

All my life, I had relied on my father for protection, and now all of a sudden, that shield was gone. My only consolation was to be extra-brilliant at everything I did, including my school work. I passed top of the class with high grades and I could now progress to university.

My father was a man of peace. My brother too is of a similar inclination. He grew up as a quiet yet strikingly funny person. However, there were these silent and unspoken ways that I learnt from him about how to survive in life. He was a strong guy too and I idolised this trait.

The pain of loss can be overwhelming. The unexpected emotions, from shock or anger to disbelief, guilt and profound sadness. They say the pain eases with time but this is not true for me. No day goes by that I do not think of my father; whether lovingly or painfully. However, it is important to find new meaning and move on with life even after a great loss.

Every day, I think of how my father never got to see me graduate, walk me down the aisle and see me become the woman he had hoped I could be. Nonetheless, that did not stop me from graduating or getting married. Yes, I do believe that the people we love do not die. They live within us. They may not speak verbally to us, and we do not see them in the flesh, but there is a special connection that keeps them alive in us.

Lesson: The Power to Persevere

"You only have the power to change yourself. When you do, do it for yourself with no expectation from others to understand or cheer you on"

Despite the struggles and the pain, despite the hurt and the brokenness, despite being broken by family, friends and those of whom I expected to protect me, it was my decision to be a victor or a victim. Only I had the power to change my life without expecting any sympathy from family or friends. My mother always said if you hear "no" for an answer, you are speaking to the wrong person.

Life is a journey to self-discovery. Self-awareness only begins with oneself and within the self. Some people go through masking who they really are. Others simply become what others want them to be, giving away their power, that is, the power to be authentically themselves. This is probably the greatest misfortune we can put ourselves in. I had to learn that this is easier said than done.

Knowing thyself is a classic saying that continues to offer a valuable reminder today. It is only through the discovery of the self that we can identify our purpose and actualize our potential. On the other hand, failure to embark on a pilgrimage of self-discovery cheats us of the opportunity to understand who we are and what we want out of life, as well as how we can help others during our time on this earth.

There is no perfect way to self-discovery but one can strive for excellence and do the best that they can at any given time. The most important thing is to put in the work. By acknowledging that we need to change and by understanding that there is mighty greatness within us, we can slowly gravitate to the better life we seek. Set aside time to truly reflect on your life. Be in the moment, be present and watch your thoughts deeply. Take a personal inventory. Reflect on the following questions: What have you accomplished? Do you have any major fears? Are you struggling against certain obstacles? Have you set realistic goals? Do you enjoy occasional daydreams or fantasies?

Embrace the journey to self-discovery. You may feel anxious, nervous, or even afraid of what you could find deep within. Don't worry. Whatever lies hidden in your soul can be the light of discovery. You can grow even stronger by honestly facing the facts revealed by your personal inventory. Don't be afraid to admit who you are and accept your limitations. Only then can you start working on the weaknesses to become a better person and enjoy your strengths to savour each day.

The key to one's happiness should always be safeguarded by oneself. When you are full of happiness and joy, you will attract more happiness and joy. Think about your physical being. If you could be healthier, for example, by losing a few pounds or developing a fitness routine, start planning your lifestyle changes. Set reasonable goals, such as losing two pounds per month, and stick with it. Or start walking 10 minutes daily and increase that amount of time by 10 minutes each week until you can walk for an hour. (However, get your doctor's consent before making specific changes like these.)

The mistake we all make is focusing on the outside while the real work needed rests within us. We focus on losing weight or gaining a muscle, whitening our teeth, or tightening our face. But the real solutions lie with how we relate to and treat each other, being grateful and always giving, with no expectation of return.

Getting to know yourself, just like getting acquainted with anyone, takes time. Don't expect to find out everything there is to know in a few hours. Be prepared to go the distance through a series of activities and reflections. The ultimate enlightenment will be worth it.

The journey of self-discovery is like no other trip you will ever take. It can be an immensely exciting and satisfying experience. Refraining from comparing yourself with other people is paramount. Comparison breeds condemnation. It is acceptable to draw inspiration from others but not to a point of wishing for their life. It is important that one remains authentic to oneself because God made us to be different with great reason and purpose. He made us unique and different, and that's the beauty of humanity. It is therefore important that we realise that the power to happiness lies within us and that the onus is on us to pursue a joyful life. In everything we do, we should consider ourselves adequate and sufficient. This way, we look for the answers or happiness we need from within ourselves rather than from without.

1996, Form 1, Ramoja CJSS

At home, Moroka Village

University of Botswana

With my kids at The Capitol,
Washington DC

UN Headquarters, New York
City

Part 3

PERSEVERANCE

The Call

It was in the fall of 2006 when I received a call that would change my life forever:

Ms Zebe: Good morning, Angelinah. This is Zebe calling you from the Ministry of Education.

Me: Good morning, Ms. Zebe.

Ms Zebe: I am calling you to let you know that you have been selected for the commonwealth scholarship in the UK for September 2007.

At this point, I was sobbing quietly, words failing to come out of my mouth.

Ms Zebe: You will have to come to our office on Friday for the next procedure. Please bring your birth certificate and passport. Thank you. Bye

Me: Will do so. Thank you.

In disbelief, I wondered if my dreams were coming true at last.

I had just graduated with a first class degree from the University of Botswana that October. At the time of the call, I was interning at a library under the auspices of one of the best parastatals in the country, a research institute called the Botswana Institute for Development Analysis (BIDPA).

I remember trying to be calm as though this kind of opportunity was expected. I looked around me to see if anyone had heard my conversation on the phone because the phone call seemed too good to be true. Since I was in the library, I had to muster my self-control. I ran outside to the parking lot. There, I sobbed, danced and prayed so hard. If there is something that I have inherited from my mother, it is the habit of praying. I believe prayer from my mother moves mountains. This is because of the way I saw her praying. I always look forward to my mother's prayers.

So when I received this joyful news, the only thing that came to my mind was to pray. I meditate and pray for anything, even when in awkward situations. My favourite verse in the Bible is Philippians 4:6, which reads:

"Don't worry about anything but pray about everything. With thankful hearts offer up your prayers and requests to God."

It doesn't matter what I could be going through; this verse gets me through.

The phone call and all the drama surrounding me happened in the reading room of the BIDPA library. I remember my classmates, Pearl and Fiona, whom I was interning with at the library, looking at me like I was crazy.

I tried to keep it down but the tears of joy kept pouring out of my eyes. They could not tell if the news that I had received was good or bad. I bet my dance was so weird and it confused them more. They could not tell if it was a happy dance or a sad one. I had kept them in suspense for a little while as I prayed and danced confusingly. I said, "Ladies, I am going to the UK. God is great". I could see the confusion on their faces. Their eyes were fixed on me as they silently digested what I had just said.

Once I had explained and they understood everything, they each gave me a big hug and wished me well. They were very happy for me. But they cautioned me to follow through very well and make sure it was not a scam. Both Pearl and Fiona were older than me, although they were my classmates so I respected their opinions as my big sisters.

NOT SO ROSY

Once the excitement was over, my emotions rose. My life soon became a roller coaster of emotions as it dawned on me that I was pregnant. What was supposed to be the happiest moment of my lifetime; winning a prestigious scholarship, became a source of all sorts of emotions, from panic, fear, anxiety and sadness to anticipation and excitement. Never ever in my life have I experienced all sorts of emotions at the same time.

I wondered what would happen to my baby if I was to end up in the UK studying. Was I ready for the separation with my new-born? As the timeline indicated, my daughter would be only five months old the following year when I started school. I was afraid, I was anxious, I was angry, I was depressed and honestly, I was just a wreck.

But I had to place my fears aside and soldier on. This was not a self-pity party. This was life unfolding right in front of me. It was another chapter to the next level, a step towards the unknown. The fear of the unknown, the fear of unchartered territory was so tangible I could not ignore it. It was insane but deep down my heart, there was this part of me that said I did not want to be anything else either than me. If this path, this opportunity was leading me to me, then let it be.

I remembered one of my mentor's words years before when he said, "Courage doesn't mean you are not afraid. Courage means you don't let fear stop you." I could tell now what he meant. Earth is a difficult place. It took courage and faith to venture into the unknown and I had to be strong and stretch my limits. Courage means our actions are not controlled by our doubts.

I have seen this so many times in my mother, a woman who no matter what you threw at her, came out of the situation better, stronger and victorious.

My mother deserted a polygamous marriage for greener pastures and found love in my dad. I saw her hurting for abandoning her young children because she had left suddenly and in fear. Seeing her deal with that pain and still finding purpose in that pain, gave me the courage I have today. She taught me that it is not the pain that counts, but it is finding the purpose and power in the pain. What you do with the pain will either make or break you.

Watching my mother sitting in her pain and coming out on the other side victorious, taught me that pain is here to make you, to form you, to cleanse and strengthen you. Find a higher purpose in your pain. Never let your pain go to waste. To this day, I credit my mother for unconsciously showing me how to deal with my pain and turning all my failures into teachers.

THE PLAN

As I began to hit the ground running, the resistance and push back I got was astonishing. The shame and the blame, the disbelief and rejection, the doubt, the regret and every negative thought welled up in me, threatening to suffocate me. Every day, I would cry myself to sleep.

On the night of April 11th 2007, I went into labour. My water broke three weeks earlier, right on time for the estimated date of arrival of the baby, April 12th. Honestly, I really had no business becoming a mom at that particular time. All I really needed was time, time to get my life on track. I needed to be in the UK, get my Master's degree and get my mind and life right.

But babies don't wait. They come when they are ready, even if their parents are not. I wasn't married. I wasn't even in a relationship any longer with my baby's father. I had no family nearby. I had been laid off from my temporary job at BIDPA Library. I had gotten this temporary job right after graduating college. My mom was all the way in Moroka Village. My college friends were trying to figure out their lives after graduating. I had my church family, very great church friends, some pretty awesome ones. But I didn't want to be an imposition to anyone.

Despite the challenges, I would wake up every morning and think, "Thank God for life. Thank God for this baby. I have my degree. That's more than a lot of people in my spot have. I should be able to overcome this." I wanted to remain positive and strong for my baby girl. Parenting wasn't something that I was thinking of. The only thing on my mind was school. Hopefully one day I could be a better parent.

Theoentle Anita finally arrived at 8:35 a.m. on April 12, 2007. She was so little and so precious, that I immediately felt the connection when the nurses finally brought her to me. It had been a very complicated labour and I thought she needed my protection. It wasn't hard to love her. She was quiet, beautiful and full of grace. The parenting instinct immediately kicks in.

So, I set her in her plastic crib and just put my head in my hands and cried. I was no longer alone but I was feeling that way more than ever. The father of my new-born had not bothered to call or come to see the baby and me. Tears started dropping and I didn't try to keep them in.

Once I had released all my pain, I took another look at my baby girl, asleep, swaddled, perfect. She was 2.7 kg half, with lungs much stronger than I had anticipated. She was on the chubby side. You could tell, this would be a big baby. She was perfect.

My panic suddenly switched to that of gratitude. I felt lucky for having a healthy baby. Lucky for having wonderful friends and family, even if they were helping me from afar. Lucky that my sister, at seven months pregnant herself, had left her home to be with me during the first few days of the birth of my baby. My sister is another stronghold and pillar in my life.

Receiving a gift that I wasn't ready for became the very thing I needed most. My daughter is probably the best thing that happened to me when I least expected.

Ever since our breakup, the father of my child had never called or checked on me. This is the coldest person I had ever met in my life. He lived in a mining town, Orapa, in Botswana, about six hours from the capital city, Gaborone. We had met in Gaborone as strangers but it was love at first sight. I was a student at the University of Botswana. He was already working as a mine foreman at this mining town. I would visit him whenever it was convenient. Every time I visited, I sensed his toxic behaviours and habits, his values that did not match mine and yet I ignored my gut instinct. Then he truly revealed himself after I had told him I was pregnant.

Clearly, he was not ready to be a father. Throughout our relationship, I was exhausted emotionally. I became numb to the feeling that I was going to be hurt. I did not know how

114

deep this hurt would affect me. The soldier in me blocked out all unpleasantness and thought somehow we would be alright.

Despite the pain and the hurt, he became my last resort. I could not bear the thought of being homeless when he had shelter. I thought of going to Orapa, not to be with him but to have a safe place for the few critical weeks before and after the birth of my daughter.

Two weeks before my due date, I boarded a bus from Gaborone to Orapa. He was unaware of my impending visit and I was unconcerned about the fact that I would require a permit to allow me entrance into the mining compound. Orapa mine in Botswana is a country within a country. It is the only town in Botswana that has 24hr protection and is only accessible with a permit. As a citizen of Botswana, one needs to apply for a visa(permit) to get into town. It is fenced from end to end and very secure. In order to get into this town, if you are not an employee or a close relative of an employee, someone has to invite you in and apply for your visa. That person becomes responsible for your conduct while in Orapa.

Since I had not informed my boyfriend that I intended to visit, I did not have a permit but I boarded the six- hour bus anyway. This was by far, one of the worst adult decisions of my life. The long ride and all the painful memories associated

115

with it, is the reason I detest buses to this day. I felt anxious and scared throughout that trip and the uncertainties ahead of me made my heart heavier. For six hours, I probably stood up once halfway into the journey for a pit stop. I had brought water and a banana with me. I had no appetite for anything, and I was bordering on depression.

The entrance at Orapa mine is like that of a port of entry. All passengers in public transport are required to get off the bus, get their permit and show it to the security guard. As we approached the gate, anxiety hit me. What if I am sent back? It's almost 9pm, it's dark. If I am turned down, where do I go? What do I do, 38 weeks pregnant?

 I walked boldly to the security gate for processing. I did not utter a word; I just gave this man my identity card. He looked at me, once, twice and said, "You know you have no permit, right? Your last application was 6 months ago. Why are you here?" Those words still haunt me to this day. This guy is asking me the same questions I am asking myself, I thought. Why am I here? I really did not know.

My situation must have been written all over my face. In my distress, the universe sent a message to me through him. He gave me a permit to admit me for a day, risking losing his job. In my silence, I prayed for my good fortune and for this man's kindness.

To this day, I do not know what moved him but he had suddenly stood up, walked to his computer and fumbled around before printing a day pass without further questions. This certainly was the universe watching over me because this was an offense that could have lost him his employment.

Little did I know that there were more hurdles ahead. There is a saying in Setswana that, "Nko e re e rwele hela ha e dubelele", meaning, "We have this nose, but it doesn't predict or sniff the future". When I got my day permit, I couldn't care less about how it would be renewed. Procedurally, I had to be out of the Orapa town in 24hrs or renew the permit. Renewing the permit meant my host had to do it. Well, at that point, all I cared about was gaining access to Orapa. Sometimes one needs to take the first step and let the universe take care of the rest.

With my one-day permit in my hand, I headed to my estranged baby-daddy's townhouse. All houses in Orapa belong to the mine and employees are offered accommodation within the compound. Here I was, at his door and he had no idea about it all. At this point, my mind was set. There was no point of return. His car was parked outside, a sign that he might be home. However, sometimes he used company transport to get to work. I rang the bell twice. Whatever stood behind that door didn't matter anymore. After the second ring, the door opened, the lights burst into life and I saw a tall dark shadow of someone inside. It was him.

Him, looking extremely shocked: "Hi, Angie, what brings you here at this time?"

After a huge sigh and a moment's pause...

Him: *"Come in".*

Suddenly as I glanced up at him. The few awkward seconds felt like a lifetime. I was petrified. My heart was pumping so hard, the adrenaline rush so real I could pee on myself. What do I say to this guy? Why am I here? This is a person who hasn't seen me in almost five months. He had never bothered to call me, neither had I. And here I am, at his door, at midnight. I would freak out.

All of sudden, the baby kicked in my protruding tummy. Throughout the six-hour journey on the bus, I had not felt the baby move, now it suddenly kicked. I touched my tummy as if to calm the baby. As all this was happening, it began to drizzle. I was now getting a little wet and I slowly walked into the house, carefully wiping off the drops of rain from my face. I took a deep breath, a sigh of relief after a long journey. At this point, all I needed was a hot shower and a bed to sleep in.

Since I had been in this house before, I knew my way around. It was a small one bed-roomed affair with an open space living area, dining-room and kitchen. I had a small bag with only my maternity dress and a few other things. I thought of putting my bag in the bedroom. As I was heading there, he slowly pulled me aside.

His face turned red, and he started to breathe heavily. I thought I was in trouble. In a quiet, calm voice, he said, "Someone is sleeping in that room". I innocently inquired who would be sleeping in his bed and why they would be there. I had forgotten I had no business being there.

Clearly, I had no idea why I was asking him these questions. He might have made me pregnant, but that did not mean he was ready to be a father or let alone, be with me.

In the confusion and commotion in the living room, a woman came out of the bedroom, fully dressed and walked out of the door. He tried to talk to her, the only words I heard were, "You never told me she was pregnant". She had disappeared into the wet darkness outside and I did not care about her or him.

119

I had come to stay with Shana knowing that this was my last month of pregnancy. I had to put on a brave face. I masked all the pain, the confusion and the fear of uncertainty which woke up with me every day. I willed myself to soldier on with determination and faith that I would somehow overcome. Each day, I had to rise above my pain, my confusion, my fear and my anxiety. I had seen my mother do this and I knew, what doesn't kill me makes me stronger.

I could not bring this child into this world, especially in the first few months of her life, on the streets when the father had a home. This was the biggest decision of my life. When someone says they don't want you, believe them the first time. I had never been more hurt in my life than the few weeks I stayed with this man waiting for the arrival of my daughter. He would go for days and leave me alone at 38 weeks pregnant. I felt abandoned and hopeless.

Rejection is the worst form of mental abuse one can experience, let alone having to face it every day when heavily pregnant. To this day, I do not know how I survived that trial. He was not a violent person physically but his verbal and emotional abuse were worse than any cruelty I had endured before. I did not know what I had done to this man to deserve such treatment. The thought of raising a fatherless daughter was haunting to me.

Even after experiencing my first unplanned pregnancy during college, I felt dismayed when I saw those two tiny blue lines pop up almost eight years later. I felt like I had let myself down. When we find ourselves in the same situation repeatedly as a result of our preconditioned responses, it is important that we take a pause and reflect deeply before making any permanent choices. Usually, when we do this, change is inevitable. Be honest with yourself and how you feel!

I do not speak for everyone or believe there is a single approach to dealing with the unexpected. I do, however, have a few defensive mechanisms for anyone who might find themselves in a predicament similar to the one I was in.

The moral of this story is that not every struggle is a waste. Tough situations are lessons and an opportunity to grow. It is not where you are in life that matters, it is who you are with. You can have a roof over your head with other people, and yet still feel alone. All this time I kept my faith and prayers as I waited for the baby.

I knew I had a purpose in this universe that had to manifest itself. I dared to stay on course no matter the labels the world was giving me. Everything that I was going through at this time was preparing me for who I was to become and to live an authentic me.

POVERTY

I must admit, poverty is one of the worst forms of violence to humanity. Like racism and prejudice, poverty is not natural. It has no place amongst humanity. Everyone deserves a decent life. Ending Poverty should be at the top of any agenda that speaks of humanity. Ending poverty starts with society taking responsibility for communities by exploring innovative and sustainable ways of tackling poverty. Every human being deserves to live with full dignity.

As a society, we tend to look to the government alone to tackle poverty. If governments alone were able to eradicate poverty, they would have done so by now. Instead, the onus is on each of us to see how we can best serve our communities. We all need to stand up for ourselves and our societies. It has to be a collective and affirmative effort from everyone to end poverty.

With time, I began the process of preparing for what would be the biggest move of my life. Part of the preparations involved making sure that my children were taken care of. My mother became my guardian angel.

LESSONS

GIVE YOURSELF TIME

Every woman is different, and every situation is different. But as the old adage goes, time heals wounds, so my advice would be to relax and control your emotions. Rushing into any decision could prove to be detrimental. My decision to move in with Shana was catastrophic. It still haunts me today. Had I paused and sought clarity before making that decision, I would have saved myself the pain and heartache.

FOCUS ON THE POSITIVES

Instead of focusing on everything that seems wrong about the situation, it is better to look for positives. For me, that would have meant focusing on the beautiful gift that God had blessed me with. I could have looked forward to motherhood and tried to enjoy the pregnancy knowing that there are others who are barren and who would give anything to be in my position. I could have chosen to be enthusiastic about my then pending move to the United Kingdom.

When I revisit my situation now, I realise that it was made worse by my own self-limiting beliefs and fears. It was not as bad as I made it out to be.

SURROUND YOURSELF WITH SUPPORT.

The issue of unwanted pregnancy is not a matter that one must face alone. You may be surprised to know that more than half of all pregnancies around the world at any given time are unplanned, and most of the time, least welcomed by the parents to be. For those who keep the pregnancy, motherhood is not a dead-end but rather, a phase in the life-cycle of women.

Be very selective about who you choose to confide in. Some people, even the closest of friends, may be waiting for your next misstep so that they can laugh at your pain. Keeping positive energy and positive people is imperative. More importantly, it is from the power within that we must draw strength from during times of weakness. It provides the power to rediscover one's purpose and move forward in life.

DO NOT GIVE UP ON YOUR DREAMS.

It is never too late to restart and follow your dreams. Whatever one has to do, there is no reason to put one's dreams to rest. Life changes will occur and when there are children involved, things may seem more difficult. This, however, should not cause one to cower from their dreams. If anything, it should be motivating to pursue the best life one desires.

Everything will take time and the process may be excruciating but one must not fear the challenges of pursuing dreams as a mother. It is different and unique but it does not make anything impossible. We are our dreams and the only way to feel fulfilled is when we strive to achieve our purpose.

LET GO

I once listened to Oprah Winfrey talking about letting go and the power of forgiveness. Oprah's definition of forgiveness is, "Giving up the hope that the past could have been any different". This definition is important. Oprah's definition, for me, was powerful as it resonated well with what I had experienced. It allowed me to reclaim my power and be in control of the situation. I learnt that forgiveness and letting go has nothing to do with the other person. It is about oneself. Forgiveness is therefore a gift to the self.

It has little to do with what or how it might have transpired. It has nothing to do with the subsequent result or with the actions of the other party. It is merely letting go of what you had hoped could be.

Part 4

HELLO NEW YORK CITY

"Grew up in a town that is famous as a place of movie scenes
Noise is always loud, there are sirens all around and the streets are
mean

If I can make it here, I can make it anywhere, that's what they say

Seeing my face in lights or my name in marquees found down on
Broadway.

Even if it's not all it seems, I got a pocketful of dreams
Baby I'm from New York
Concrete jungle where dreams are made of
There's nothing you can't do
Now you're in New York
These streets will make you feel brand new
Big lights will inspire you
Hear it for New York, New York, New York"

(Alicia Keys, Empire State of Mind)

"This city will eat you alive!" If you're a New Yorker, you are quite familiar with this phrase. I came to quickly learn how true this very phrase is. Each day, ever since arriving in New York, I was gobbled up by fierce yellow taxis and hungry subways, only to be spit back into this non-stop, wild, noisy and exhilarating city. This is a city like no other. One minute you are excited and the next minute you are exhausted and overwhelmed.

To this day, I cannot clearly tell you how I feel about this city. Whether as a student or a worker, or even a Wall Streeter, you are more than likely on your way to the underground train which they call here, the subway, for transport from point A to point B. This is the easiest and fastest way to get around the city. Not the funniest or cleanest form of transport but surely you can get a lot done using the subway than the bus. Otherwise, you walk like a New Yorker. My longest walk was around twenty blocks from 42nd Street and 1st Avenue to the New York-Presbyterian Hospital on 72nd and York Avenue.

My first time on the subway I felt like an idiot. First, when I arrived at the subway stop, I observed visitors like me struggling with the ticket vending machines or kiosks, to obtain a metro card, which is the ticket that allows you entry into train or station. I observed New Yorkers giving directions to hopelessly lost souls and assisting strangers in diverse ways. Having to carry your luggage up more than twenty staircases, is a strenuous exercise and that is what I had to do on my arrival in New York. Elevators or lifts are rarely functional, so I had no other choice.

From 4pm sunsets in the winter to oversized pizza slices, I had always imagined what it would be like to live and work in the greatest city in the world, the Big Apple, New York City. I had imagined commuting on the 6 a.m. train, from the Bronx to Brooklyn and grabbing my morning Starbucks coffee, as well as jogging in the famous Central Park. I dreamed about the adrenaline of being a part of this melting pot, a city that knows no curfews and never sleeps. Slowly my imagination became my reality.

It had been two months after I had received my offer letter for a job at the United Nations that this award winning song got released. This became my introduction to New York, *Empire State of Mind*. A city that knows no boundaries. This is a city of dichotomies, a melting pot of cultures and the most exhausting and exhilarating place on earth.

People say it is the hardest city to live in, so if you can survive New York, you can survive anywhere. Whether you're a regular visitor to the Big Apple, or you're on your maiden visit, you can never exhaust the richness and the beauty of this city.

Twenty years ago, if you would have told me New York was on my list of places to visit or let alone live in, I would have told you that you need an appointment with the doctor, you are out of your mind.

Four months after that offer letter, I set off for New York. As the air bus turned to land at JFK International Airport from O.R Tambo, that chilly morning in January, sixteen hours later and a thousand miles away, I looked out of the window and caught a glimpse of Ms. Liberty, standing there majestically as if she was sending me a sign to be still.

As scared as I was, the sight of Ms. Liberty stirred something in my tummy as if it was a sign from the universe proclaiming, I am with you. I arrived in America with $289 in my bank account and a carry-on bag. A friend in the UK had paid for a week of my accommodation at the YMCA on 47th street, Midtown.

However, I didn't know how long the $289 would last me. All I knew was that, as everyone had warned me, New York is expensive. The uncertainty of not knowing where my next meal would come from was a little scary. At the back of my mind was the fear of having to end up on the streets of the Big Apple. A confusion of questions swirled in my mind: What if I get lost in this strange place? Who will ever find me? What will happen to my children?

But in hindsight, there was really nothing to fear. I was in a better situation compared to other foreigners. At least I had a job and a roof over my head. I had flown in business class into this country and this was an opportunity to be grateful for. I just had to show up at work, open a US bank account and my salary would be deposited into that account. It was only a matter of showing up for my first day, getting all my paperwork done and I was out of my HR office with a bank card, ready to take on New York City.

But before then, my dear sister, Nthisana, had given me written instructions on the directions from JFK to Grand Central station, and from the Grand Central Station to the hotel YMCA. Now that I am a New Yorker, I feel very stupid for taking a taxi from Grand Central to YMCA, midtown. This a five-minute walk from where the JFK shuttle bus begins.

I went through immigration at JFK airport like I had been there before. I was now getting used to airports, having travelled to the UK and Europe as a student. The YMCA would be my home for a few weeks before I found my footing in the city. Every time I chance to pass there now, I smile at how it now looks different.

THIS IS WEIRD

After a week in New York City, I started noticing weird things. Of special note was the noise of the fire trucks and the buses. There is always a fire truck, emergency ambulance or police car heading somewhere. This was New York City after 9/11. I had never lived in a city with such a busy life yet life still seemed to go on unperturbed by this fuss.

Another weird thing was when I went to eat. I am a foodie. I noticed these massive food portions that I couldn't finish on my own. Then I didn't know of the doggie bag. Where I come from, you don't really take out your leftovers when eating out. I watched all that food go to waste. In my mind, a kid in Africa could use this food. One thing I can never understand about America is why the prices on the menu or shelves are misleading. The listed prices do not include tax and for restaurants, there is 20% tip policy. It's almost taboo to leave a restaurant without tipping. Please do not ask me how the tip is calculated. It's a chapter of its own.

One day I entered a restaurant and found a seat. A waitress spotted me and with a sprightly gait, made her way towards my table. She cheerfully asked me what drink I would take, and I said, "Tea". When she said, with ice or no ice, that is when I thought this city was strange. Iced tea was something I had never heard of before. I had mixed emotions as I waited for my tea, not iced. So, tea can be consumed cold? Why had I spent all my life making all those fires to brew hot tea in a hot climate? Is it that my people didn't know that tea could be consumed cold? I was flabbergasted.

In New York City, you are considered a danger if you smile at or talk to a stranger, especially on the subway. In Botswana, we make friends in our commute to work. In fact, it is considered strange and unfriendly not to greet or strike up a conversation with fellow passengers on public transport. I remember my commutes from the University of Botswana to check on my son. I would pray for a pleasant and joyful neighbour on that five-hour journey. You can actually make true friendships on the long commutes.

In New York City however, it is suspect when someone greets you or let alone, acknowledges you. In fact, when you greet people on the subway, you become a suspect. People either walk away from you because they can't trust you and your motive or you get the cold shoulder treatment.

I thought this was the most unfortunate thing humanity should ever experience, the ability not to interact freely with each other, especially on the subway. I found this cold treatment on the planes as well. I can understand we are strangers, but if we are to sit together on a five to nine-hour journey, we might be decent enough to say hello.

The other weird thing I still do not understand to this day about New York City, and I have made it my mission to rebel against, is that black remains the new black. Everywhere you look it's dark, everyone is wearing black. Interestingly, my favourite colour is white. If I was to wear my all-white in New York, I would probably attract uncalled for attention. I was surprised that in a city with a reputation of fashion, black is the most creative thing New Yorkers ever wear.

Also, New Yorkers think that cabbage is a flower and is appropriate for decorating their concrete jungle streets. They have made it their mission to find every variety of cabbage available to decorate their sidewalks. I can only imagine one reason; cabbage is forgiving and can thrive in the winter. And some of the best food you will ever eat in this city is sold on the street and on trucks.

And finally, the sun rises at 4 a.m. in the summer.

After all is said and done, the weight of New York City blissfully rests on your shoulders. And I came to realize that the city of lights, dreams, and opportunities was my new home. I grasped that Ms. Liberty was my neighbour, and that I resided in the city where artists have been cultivated, where every desire and aspiration seems to be an attainable goal and I could wander through Madison Avenue instead of a huge shopping mall. I could pass through Times Square and grab a bite, walk to a Broadway show and just live the city life.

There is a story behind every decision to migrate. People migrate for different reasons; economic, social, political or environmental. Mine just happened. I had never planned it in any way. The universe had conspired and aligned with my energy.

Where is Roosevelt Island?

Every day I felt like a tourist although I was harassed by the fear of height and water. The iconic red Roosevelt Island tram, which runs every 7 to 15 minutes to and from 59th Street and 2nd Avenue in Manhattan, made me face this fear. I made it my choice of transport to enter the Island, and during my commute to work.

When I decided to take up a new assignment at the UN headquarters in New York from the Geneva office, my friend offered her place as accommodation. She happened to live on Roosevelt Island, NY, 10044. At that time, I was oblivious of what it was like on the Island. I had heard many conspiracy theories but had never had the interest to find out.

Is Roosevelt Island haunted?

A few weeks after arriving on the Island, I found myself signing a lease in the asylum landmarked the Octagon in the Octagon rotunda. Overlooking the beautiful Upper East Side and the East River, this was a real New York dream. This is how I choose to remember the Island. The Four Freedoms State Park at the southernmost tip is a must-see and is the first memorial to the island's namesake, President Franklin D. Roosevelt, in his home state. Living on Roosevelt Island could be seen as a so-close-but-yet-so-far scenario. The Island is so close to Manhattan yet it feels so disconnected to the chaos and the mess in the city. It's more peaceful.

At the northern end of Roosevelt Island is Lighthouse Park, where there is ample grass, picnic tables and grills, and a historic 50-foot-tall lighthouse built by the same architect who designed the Smallpox Hospital. I spend a lot of time here with my friends in the summer barbeque.

Is the island haunted? There's a damn good chance. Known as Blackwell's Island until 1921, it was home to several hospitals, a prison and the 1834-built New York City Lunatic Asylum, which were all well-documented as having horrific conditions for those housed there. In the southern part of Roosevelt Island are the landmarked ruins of the Smallpox

Hospital, which opened in 1856 to keep the highly contagious patients from infecting the rest of the city.

What I miss most about my 10 River Road, apt 21C is the view of the city from the comfort of my home. I could watch all the ferries pass by as well as the New York City skyline and the busy Queens borough bridge. The most beautiful were nights when the city lights were on. It was the most breath-taking view I had ever seen. Not to mention that I was in my living-room.

For a long time, I had resisted the urge to leave the house unless it was a beach vacation or a trip to Hawaii. I felt very grateful. Not many people get to live like tourists each day. From the breath-taking view in the comfort of my living-room to riding the ferry or the tram commuting to work.

THE MOVE

It was a very beautiful sunny September day when I landed at Manchester Airport, in the year 2007. The University of Sheffield had arranged a meet-and-greet for international students right at the airport. We would be transported from the airport to Sheffield.

As I paced through terminal 3 of Manchester airport, I could feel my heart pounding so hard at the thought of what was going on. I was overwhelmed with fear as reality dawned on me that I had just landed in a foreign country where I knew no one and I was about to get into a bus to continue further into the abyss. I was breaking inside. This was my breakdown moment. Two things came into my mind. I could decide right there to call the police and report myself missing, or I could get into the bus and head to Sheffield. I remembered the voices of all those who had doubted my capabilities and those who had thought me insane. I suddenly felt overwhelmed with emotions.

I had to face my greatest fear yet, the fear of the unknown. This was to be the moment that would define me.

The ride on the bus to Sheffield University took about an hour. It was the most magical and beautiful bus ride I had ever taken. The fact that I was on a bus with four other students and our guide, all of whom were Asian, gave me reassurance that I was doing the right thing. My faith was energized with the assurance that God would not take me this far to leave me stranded in a foreign continent. I could not understand why the University would send a whole bus to pick up only four students. Where was everyone else?

That was the beginning of my adventure, especially when it came to the orderliness of British transportation. Where I come from, the bus does not leave until every seat is occupied. Here we were, with a whole bus to ourselves. I felt very special. Especially since I am not a fan of bus rides.

In the distance, I could see the breath-taking Yorkshire Dales and the captivating mountains and hills of the British countryside. It looked like a postcard. I had never seen such beautiful, manicured, green landscapes. This was the first time I had felt the guilt of leaving my children and my family behind. I wished they were here to experience this beauty.

None of my immediate family members had ever been to Europe. None had flown before. I was the first of my father's children to graduate in high school. I was the first to obtain a university degree. Now I had become the first to fly overseas. I could feel it, my life was about to change in a different and positive way. I knew it then and I relish it now.

An hour later, we arrived at Western Bank, Sheffield University. I had only one bag that had my first month's supplies. It was therefore easy for me to move around. I headed to the International Students Welcome Desk for my welcome package. I received all the information I needed for the week. I was already late for the orientation and first week's registration. I had delayed leaving home so I could spend much time with my new-born baby.

As a Commonwealth scholar, I had the best opportunities. My scholarship had provision for my first stipend in cash on arrival at Manchester airport. I was covered financially for a month. The first night in a B&B was tough. It was cold. I was alone and scared to death, yet I kept a brave face.

That same night, I went to a payphone and called my mother, so that she would be aware of my safe arrival in Sheffield. I told her that I had accommodation for the night and that I had taken dinner. She wanted to know everything. My mother had been worried and hearing from me was a relief to her. She had expressed reservations about my travelling to the UK. Her opinion was that I had already done well with my life and there was, therefore, no need to chase further opportunities.

She had been the first at my graduation, and no doubt it meant a lot to her.

My mother does not like travelling long distances. She has done a lot of travelling back and forth between Botswana and Zimbabwe to see her family in the past and maybe that explains her indisposition to travelling.

She had been to Gaborone a few times, and when I told her I was graduating, she had made the trip on an overnight train to see me graduate. I figured she was very proud of me. She wanted me to settle at that stage of my accomplishment so when I told her that I had received the opportunity to travel abroad to study, she simply could not understand. Thankfully, I listened to my inner self and travelled anyway.

Settling in Sheffield was tough.

I had not expected it to be easy and I know that it could have turned out even worse than it actually had. Yet nothing in my background could have sufficiently prepared me for Sheffield. The shock of having to live among people who were so different from me was great.

I strove to make the best of my new home. Everything, from the school curriculum to life after school, was different. All the mild research I had done about this society proved to be inadequate. I experienced an enormous cultural shock.

I willed myself to be open-minded and trusted myself to learn without judgement. This was the only way I could fit into this new society. I had to adjust to the English accent so that I could understand what was said. I had to grasp their mannerisms and social etiquette. I also learnt to appreciate elements from this society that I thought my people could emulate, including their orderliness and respect for time.

Some things were easy to understand, some I had to consciously recall. I was in South Yorkshire and the people here speak Yorkshire. Yes, English has dialects. I was considered to be speaking the Queen's English in an accent because my grammar was "perfect". The pain came when I had to ask my grocery store assistant for something I could not find on the shelves. Having to repeat myself five times because she couldn't understand my accent when I said "butter", was stressful. Many times I had come out of the supermarket with none of the stuff I would have wanted to buy, not because they were not there, but because of the absence of mutual comprehension between me and the store assistant.

And then there was Yorkshire Sunday roast. I am not sure if it is a British thing or just a Sheffield thing. As I began to have friends in the community, mainly from church, I got invites for Sunday lunch. My first introduction to a British home-cooked meal was Sunday roast. Sunday roast is a British meal that revolves around roast beef but which includes a series of other tasty recipes and sauces, served in the same rich and colourful dish, to celebrate Sunday together with loved ones. It is also served on important occasions, like Christmas and family gatherings. Traditionally, it's eaten around 3pm, although many now eat Sunday meals around dinner time.

When Marie, from church, invited me for a Sunday dinner, I imagined the come-dine-with-me kind of reception. For me, three months after arriving in Sheffield, this was closer to Christmas. I didn't know anyone else and she was the first Brit to host me with her family for dinner. This is probably the best memory I have of my time in Sheffield.

In order to get to Marie's house, I had to take a bus to a city called Shiregreen. It was a 15-20minute ride from where I lived in Heeley. I was told dinner was at 4pm. I arrived half an hour late and being an African, I actually thought I was early. Everyone was waiting for me and dinner was almost getting cold. I had not called to say I was running late or was unable to come, hence they had assumed I was still coming and waited. Upon arriving, I learnt later from Marie, that I had not apologized for being late. Everyone was probably piqued by this rudeness though no one had said anything.

Well, I had just acted according to my African norms not knowing how misplaced they were in my current environment. Also, being my first time around an all-white audience, I was clearly lost in a strange cultural scenario.

As we sat at the table, I observed the dinner. In the plate, along with the main course of roasted beef, were roasted vegetables – carrots and parsnips, potatoes, cooked both in the oven and as mash, peas, broccoli, cauliflower, and also pigs in blanket. And then the ubiquitous Yorkshire pudding, baked batter with a shape similar to muffins. To embellish the whole dish, including the vegetables sides, there was gravy, a thick sauce made with the juice of the meat and enriched with aromatic herbs and spices, broth and a little flour for thickness. This is the part I did not understand. So when I saw everyone pour the funny looking brown, it looked so weird I thought I would retch. This was yet another insult to the British tradition.

Marie: Angie, you have to try the gravy on your food, love.

Me: No, thank you. I will have the soup later (later to me, is never).

Marie: This is not soup. Its gravy. There is a difference between soup and gravy. You can't have roast with gravy love. (all this in a heavy Yorkshire accent).

145

I gave in and poured gravy on my food, including my pudding. I struggled to finish the meal. First of all, the beef was not as tasty as the beef in Botswana and the gravy poured over food made it hard for me to eat. Never had I seen that before. As people finished their servings and went for the second, my plate was still full until Marie urged me to eat. My food was even getting cold. You could tell Marie did not appreciate that I had hardly touched my food. Where I come from, it is rude not to finish your food. However, I could not manage this feat with this particular meal.

Coming from a country that has the best beef in the world, it was clear this was not the beef roast I had expected. To exacerbate matters, I watched the Brits serve me fish and chips. To this day, I cannot eat fish and chips without some repugnance. Whoever came up with the idea to mash pieces and put them next to fried fish must have been out of ideas. Sadly, the English breakfast in hotels doesn't translate to the one I had seen on pictures. You can see my passion for Sheffield ended when the food disappointed me. However, there is more to this beautiful city.

I spent most of my time as a student, in the beautiful 19-acre Botanical Gardens. I would go there for my afternoon strolls, just to recharge. This was especially during spring and summer when many of the plants are in full bloom. In the summer, the garden booms with many music, art, and theatrical events that are staged on the grounds. It was the best time of the year to be in the garden. Sadly, summer doesn't last that long here. Soon, it was time to pack my bags and head home after submitting my thesis.

Sheffield had introduced me to my first culture shock but it did very little to prepare me for the Big Apple. First of all, it was the language, then the food, and lastly, driving. Of course, Sheffield is England and New York is the United States of America and these are different worlds. In Sheffield, when moving a car from a parking lot, you can reverse the car, whilst in the United States, even if the gear says "R", you don't reverse. I had to learn quickly how to drive on a different side of the road.

Furthermore, in Sheffield I drank fizzy drinks but in New York, I drank soda. There is fish and chips in Sheffield, and in the US, there are French fries with ketchup, not tomato sauce.

What I found weird was how the food lacked seasoning and tabasco sauce is everywhere. I will save the conversation about tabasco for another day.

Let me tell you about my experience in Sheffield. People here do mind their own business. This was different from Moroka where everyone knows something about everyone else. This was a nuclear society where the independence and respect for the privacy of individuals, is seen as a virtue. I saw eighty-year olds drive, go shopping and even live on their own. This was civilization. In Moroka, we stayed with my grandmother before she even turned sixty because it was a necessity and obligation that defines our extended family practice.

Here in Sheffield, everyone expressed a sense of politeness. However, what I found strange was how quickly a smile could turn into cold seriousness. This was different from my people who laugh loudly, scream their greetings to passing neighbours, bellow in pain at loss and generally have warmth to spare even for strangers.

At home, meeting anyone anywhere is reason enough for a small chat. Corridors or the streets are places people tell you how they feel, the latest deaths and all varieties of gossip. Rarely do you just pass someone without greeting them or asking genuinely how they feel. And when asked there is no brushing off, people answer openly and freely?

Here, when I met classmates and lecturers on the corridors of the campus, I would wait to greet or make eye contact. However, everyone seemed too busy for greetings let alone to stop and chat. I was homesick. I missed laughing and chatting without fear of being misunderstood.

When winter arrived, it found me unprepared. It came faster and colder than expected. It got severely cold and miserable for my liking. At any rate, I had never been exposed to snow. I had not seen or experienced below zero freezing temperatures. I had never owned a heavy jacket my entire life. The heaviest jacket I had at home was a leather jacket that I used for our light desert winters in Botswana. I did not know what a snowstorm or blizzard meant.

The weather in the United Kingdom was unbelievable for me. It was then that I got to understand the Brits' obsession with the weather. There are weather updates every 10 minutes on television and whenever people meet, their greetings allude to the beauty of the weather especially when it is bright and sunny. In contrast, I had seen too many bright and shiny days in my life which I had taken for granted. To me, this was how it was supposed to be- bright, sunny, dry heat. My village was within a subtropical desert climate where it is mostly hot. I came to understand why white people I met in Botswana always had outdoor wear. They leapt at any opportunity they got to go outside and enjoy nature.

Loneliness would settle heavily on me after lectures. No one wanted to be out and about in this weather. To start with, I had few friends and therefore limited access to the greater society. My life was split between being in class and being at home.

My first Christmas was quiet. Here, a neighbour is not one's friend, but in Africa, neighbours are family. Neighbours are the first people who get an invitation to a wedding. They are the first people you talk to when faced with a problem. Neighbours, by default, are the lifeline to a happy neighbourhood. Such is the beauty of our culture. Strange as it may sound, this is our way of life. Neighbours look after each other's kids; are the default nannies and watchdogs. It is our way of life. Not what I experienced in Sheffield. For the time I lived in the UK, I never had a neighbour invite me or come for dinner. Marie was my church colleague and I did not have any acquaintance with any of my immediate neighbours.

I came to learn about life, that if it doesn't challenge you, it won't change you. Challenges teach you to overcome and when you devise new ways to overcome obstacles then you become successful. My mother and my pastors all emphasized that being out of the comfort zone is a horrible feeling, but it's also where growth comes from. There is no vision with no provision. Nothing amazing ever happens in our comfort zones. It sounds like a cliché, but that's very true.

This is my learning experience this far

Go with the decision that will make for a good, authentic you. As one of my new friends had told me, certainly now I was going to have some interesting and authentic stories to tell back home. Always be you because everyone else is busy being themselves. God never created photocopies. We are all unique in our own ways, wonderfully made and capable of being the best version of ourselves. People's perceptions should not shape your future.

Never stop learning. I have always been a curious person. I've reached a point where I never stop learning. The more you learn, the more you earn. Learning removes ignorance, and this is not only about being book-smart, it's educating ourselves about the world around us. Once you know something, you become better at how you see and do things. Ultimately this world can become a better place if everyone strived to consistently search for understanding.

Before embarking on anything new, prepare yourself carefully. I've done a lot of planning and preparation in my life. At times, it just came naturally, whilst sometimes I had to consciously search for understanding and prepare myself thoroughly. To be prepared is to be fore-armed and the inevitable anxiety, depression, and pressure can be controlled. If you aren't confident, be YOU anyway. Stay true to you.

Stay true to your values. Do what needs to be done without complaining. Complaining won't speed things up.

I also learnt that the same culture of individuality was practised in New York City and Geneva. This is a strange way of living. This made me appreciate my culture more and love my people better. Was I missing something? Our ability to love and protect all children of the community as our own should not be taken for granted. I became acutely aware that we Africans are different. It is this difference that makes us beautiful.

This beauty is still in my heart even after ten years of not living in Africa. It has been an amazing journey that has taught me more about life, love and fear than any educational or self-help book could ever teach me. It has broadened my horizon, opened my mind and has shown me diverse sides of life, people and processes. I have grown deeper and more awakened than I could ever imagine. I look at my peers who have not had the same exposure and consider myself very blessed. I had never designed my life to turn out this way, but life has worked itself out somehow.

The fairy tale I had expected to happen in my life journey in Botswana, happened while I was on the move. I often look back at what I have been through in this life and I realise that every challenge was an exercise that was meant to prepare me for greater challenges and achievements. I have learnt that perceptions do not shape the future but actions and beliefs determine destiny.

Migration can be lonely. Migration involves loss. When I left Moroka, a part of me was lost. My relationship with my family was redefined.   Their lives got disrupted – everything changed.

My son used to have a close relationship with my mother but that was disrupted by my translocation. My mother had raised China. The bond they had was so strong that he called my mother Mama. I remember my mother refusing to hand over my children. She feared for them. She did not know if they would be secure with me. She was protective because she had developed a bond with them.

Efforts to reclaim that which has been lost are usually futile, more so for those returning from exile. The losses are dire and they are constant. One misses many family milestones; from funerals and family caucuses to birthdays, graduations and weddings. These are significant events that one cannot reclaim.

One of the things I could not forgive myself for was the passing on of my grandmother while I was in Sheffield. I did not have a chance to say goodbye to my grandmother because as a student, I could not afford airfare back home. My grandmother's death was so tragic and I failed to have the closure necessary to let her go. I live in regret each day. My grandmother died in Botswana. She had been visiting my mother for the first time from her native Zimbabwe. I had financed the whole trip because I knew how important it was for both my grandmother and my mother. Yet it ended in pain. But I had to heal. Healing is intentional especially if you get to the root of the problem.

Growing up, I used to visit my grandmother in Kazangarare in Zimbabwe. I never used to understand why my grandmother did not visit us in Botswana. I later found out from my mother that my grandmother had never possessed a passport. She did have one because she could not afford to get one. I also think my grandmother disliked any travel outside of the familiar Kazangarare area. Even going to the city which was roughly 200miles away, was considered a daring affair. Imagine the courage it must have taken her to cross borders and travel for the lengthy distance into Botswana.

One morning, my mother revealed to me my grandmother's desire to visit her. She had wanted to visit since my father's death and naturally, she was also missing her daughter. My mother too had not been to Zimbabwe for years since my father's death so they both needed to see each other.

The only issue was that my mother did not have the means. She, therefore, turned to me to finance the trip. I sent her money to get a passport and a ticket to Botswana for my grandmother. She went there safely and stayed for nearly three months. On her last day before she could return to Zimbabwe, my grandmother suffered a stroke. She had sugar diabetes that had not been sufficiently monitored.

I remember my sister calling me to tell me that our grandmother was in the hospital. I had no idea what that meant. In my mind, I was certain she would be alright and she would return home. Little did I know that in no time, I was to send money to transport her body back to Zimbabwe. This was a tragedy I would have to live with. I wondered if maybe she would still be alive if she had not come to Botswana and the guilt choked me. I am, however, grateful that I managed to ensure that my mother got an opportunity to spend time with her mother before she passed on. This is the most devastating time I have ever had. I have never slept peacefully since that day. The pain of how she died still lingers in my mind. One morning I was talking to my grandmother, excited that she had come to Botswana to see her daughter and her grandchildren, the next morning she was gone, forever. What if....?

Overall, this journey has been an amazing one that has taught me more than I had expected. My life had seemed like every step I took threatened to be another epic fail. Negativity had dogged me but today, I am grateful for all the lessons, no matter how they came. Any day I would encourage anyone to dare to fail.

Failure is a set-up for success. For every setback, God is setting one up for greater and more amazing things. A child can only be born after an agonising nine months and excruciating labour pains. It is the same with life. Every beautiful thing has a price and a process. We must be willing to go through the tests and trials in order to birth our dreams.

I have sat on tables with people from around the world. I have had intimate conversations with people I could only imagine in my dreams just a few years before. I have dined and laughed with strangers. I have travelled to places I never thought I could ever go, from Buckingham Palace to the White House.

To build a new existence far away from everything you know and believe in, is the most powerful feeling in the world. In the diaspora, there are no fairy tales. Only harsh realities that demand one to put in the work or be swallowed up by the harsh realities of life.

From my experience, I have learnt these essential five things about migration. They are not a blueprint or guidelines, but they may be worth noting.

1. Your loved ones will be devastated.

No matter how you try to sugar-coat it, moving abroad is essentially a selfish choice. It is great that one can live their dreams but it threatens the family fabric and relationship with the immediate community.

2. You will feel guilty, often.

When one moves to the other side of the globe, time and financial constraints will inevitably determine the social choices one has to make. Attending a friend's wedding may prevent one from being there for one's father's 60th birthday or a sister's graduation. How to choose and justify a choice becomes a burden one must carry silently.

Despite knowing that this is my life and this is the path I have chosen to take, I still feel guilty about being far away from my mother and siblings.

3. You will feel lonely.

I have always been fortunate to be surrounded by many wonderful people. When moving to yet another country, I have not had a problem meeting people to hang out with and explore my new environs.

However, even though I was seldom alone, I did experience a deep sense of loneliness sometimes, especially in the midst of profoundly different cultures. It takes time to build meaningful relationships abroad and until then, loneliness remains constant.

4. You will not fit in back home

Moving abroad has changed me in so many ways that I could not have possibly imagined. I have discovered passions and fears I did not know I had. I have abandoned old convictions and beliefs that have ceased to serve me. It has been a great opportunity for self-discovery and I am grateful that I have managed to embrace it fully. It has also alienated me from my people and the place I call home.

It is important to realise that little or no change happens in the village. The way of life, along with the usual tradition, persists to this day. My attitude regarding most things has evolved and this may be out of sync with that of the village.

Being back at the village is always wonderful and fills me with so much joy and peace. I, however, do not fit in. Many people do not remember me and those who do, have little in common to share with me. When I move around the village, I have to introduce myself as my son's mother. They know my son and can identify me through him.

I am equally reluctant to condone some of our practices simply because I know how they can affect one's life negatively in the long run. Some of these negative effects I have experienced first-hand and am therefore willing to protect others from them. But this does not sit well with my people and sometimes it causes me to feel like an outcast.

The same is true for the newly adopted home in the diaspora. One can acclimatise well and adjust to their new society but everyone will always ask you about your roots. I have met many sojourners who struggle with the existential questions of where they belong and where they fit in. Some remain on the move because it is the human condition to search for belongingness. Yet when you have moved on, you still can no longer really fit into any community.

5. You will lose dear friends.

Friends are the backbone of one's life. They are with us through thick and thin. But with time apart from each other, even the closest of friends can eventually become distant. It is also easy to forget about their birthdays due to different time zones and busy schedules of life.

HOME IS HOME – MAKING A DIFFERENCE

"Every day is a journey, and the journey itself is home". Matsuo Basho

All my life, I have always loved helping people, and this meant coming back to Moroka Village. There is nothing that makes me happier than to see the joy on peoples' faces after you have shown kindness to them. Seeing other people happy, seeing hope rekindled and the feeling they have that they are important fulfils me. All I value is to touch peoples' lives. This has been one of my chief motivations for travelling the world. I could easily have given up in the midst of those winter storms, far away from the warmth that my body was used to. But I did not because I knew that this could be a certain way of empowering myself to help other people.

I had the same motivation far back when I was babysitting toddlers for free in the village. The joy of taking care of someone who could not do anything for me in return was fulfilling. What was even more meaningful was to see the joy of mothers when they came to pick up their children. I always felt that I had saved their day and looking back now, I think I saved lives too. For some mothers, it would probably have

160

been the only opportunity to attend to some ventures in order to earn some much-needed income for the family's upkeep.

My mission goes beyond assisting people financially. Sometimes by merely helping people to appreciate their self-worth or having a conversation with a teenager who is at the crossroads in his life makes a difference. To be able to provoke others to see better versions of themselves or seeing others inspired about life and their own dreams gives me so much joy. I am passionate about the youth, especially young girls in my home village, Moroka. I have to find ways to influence their lives positively and teach them to expect more from life.

Having travelled the world and lived in different countries, I now have a different definition of what home is. Home is what you make it to be. I have lived comfortably in Sheffield, New York, and Geneva and this has taught me that home is a process in the journey of life. I have learnt to make every city I live in, home. It does not mean that I conform to everything everywhere, it just means that I try to live as best as I can at any moment and place.

I try to make an impact on peoples' lives when I can. I remember when I was in Geneva, Switzerland, I met a lady of Kenyan-German origin and founder of the African Women in Europe. She invited me to serve as one of the administrators and event organisers with her team. I helped organise events that brought together hundreds of women of African descent, who were making a difference in their countries while in the diaspora. At a later stage, she asked me to host the organisation's radio talk show, and the outreach became even bigger. I experienced a flash-back of those days of humble beginnings when I was busy with my mother's paraffin business. Now I am teaching and sharing my knowledge with others and such acts of service bless the world.

As an immigrant working in Switzerland, I could have chosen to focus on making a living and sending money home to my family. Organizing talks would perhaps have largely benefitted the hotels from the rentals and refreshments. But because Geneva was now my new home, and this organisation had these women who were doing phenomenal things for their communities, I felt I should contribute to a noble cause.

I am also very passionate about developing talents in my country. Sport is a powerful tool for strengthening social ties, impacting lives and building communities. I strongly believe that this is in line with the historic adoption of the United Nations (UN) 2030 Agenda for Sustainable Development Goals and with the designation of April the 6th as International Day of Sports for Development and Peace. I hope that Botswana and every country embrace sports and commit to continue to use it as a tool that can eradicate poverty, especially for the youth.

I believe I am where I am today because someone gave me a chance and I got an education that opened doors for me. I want to open doors too for those girls in the village. Educating girls is educating a generation. We will achieve this by empowering the Parents Teachers Associations in schools, encouraging parents to be part of their children's education and empowering teachers to reform our education system in the process.

I have a dream to see girls lead, and grow into transformational leaders who will be at the forefront of social reform. I also pray for leaders who trust in and honour God's calling and work for the good of their communities. It is my hope that every African child will one day be branded for success.

FINAL THOUGHTS

Life becomes meaningful when others can smile because you made them smile. There are good and kind people in this world. If you can't find one, be one! Be authentic. Be You. Be the reason someone believes in the good of the world.

Those who live only for themselves, limit their potential to transcend any limitations in their lives. Those who live only for themselves are actually against themselves. If you can't be on your side, how can anyone else be on your side? Love and respect yourself enough to be on your side. Refuse to be a dead-end and be a fountain! Never underestimate the difference you can make in the lives of others. This can be your legacy.

Success in life isn't just about what you 've accomplished for yourself; it's about what you inspire others to accomplish. You can never look good trying to make others look bad. You rise by lifting others. This is the legacy we all need to strive for. When you live a life with a purpose, a life that strives to improve others, your life in turn improves. Plant a seed, nurture a seed and prepare the ground for production and harvest. More importantly, live your best life. A life that is full of love, compassion, empathy and looks for the good in others. This world needs more good people. Be the good that becomes of society.

The End

Other Books and Publications

"The United Nations Library is Seriously Social" by Angelinah C. Boniface, Dag Hammarskjöld Library, The United Nations, New York in Using Social Media in Libraries Best Practices, CHARLES HARMON AND MICHAEL MESSINA -editors.

"Migration and Culture Preservation" Culture Celebrating Diversity: Sharing Positive of Migration

" Born a Migrant; my story" in The Perfect Migrant: How to Achieve a Successful Life in Diaspora

Acknowledgement

I am grateful to God for making this book possible. To my family for all the dinners I missed while trying to make this happen. To my friends who edited my work, I will forever be grateful. Thank you.

About the Author

Ms Angelinah Boniface Kegakilwe is a mother, wife and an International Civil Servant at the United Nations (UN). She started her work at the UN Headquarters in 2010, having completed the National Recruitment Examinations (NCE) process. She has since been to Geneva, Switzerland and is currently in New York for her second tour of duty.

Ms Boniface has co-authored a book titled *The Perfect Migrant: How to Achieve a Successful Life in the Diaspora*. The book is an intriguing and captivating anthology authored by people who are not commonly associated with the term "migrant". Her second book contribution was in 2018, and is entitled *Celebrating Diversity: Sharing Positive Stories of Migration Around the World*. Ms Boniface continues to inspire others about the power of celebrating the diversity of people

Ms. Boniface also contributed a chapter entitled, the United Nations Library is seriously social, in a book Using Social Media in Libraries, Best Practices, edited by Charles Harmon and Michael Messina.

She is very passionate about the challenges and issues that affect the girl child and youth. She works on various projects which include youth empowerment programmes, human rights, community development, leadership training and sports.

Her recent project held at Moroka Village was a themed football tournament that brought together over three hundred youths for fun and business. The idea of this event was to use sports to empower the youth.

As a mother to a daughter, Ms Boniface is a passionate advocate for issues that affect women. She has contributed and initiated several projects that empower women and girls, including raising funds for her former primary school in Moroka.

For all your feedback and comments, get in touch with the Author on:

Botswana: +26775451406

Zimbabwe: +263775102051

USA: +16468949964

UK: +447786722531

Or

Email: abc.amazonbooks@gmail.com

A BILLIONAIRE PUBLISHERS PRODUCTION

Made in the USA
Middletown, DE
21 February 2021